Tales from
Star Lake

Sin and skulduggery
among brothers
of the angle

MEREO
Cirencester

Mereo Books

1A The Wool Market Dyer Street Cirencester Gloucestershire GL7 2PR
An imprint of Memoirs Publishing www.mereobooks.com

Tales from Star Lake: 978-1-86151-765-4

First published in Great Britain in 2017
by Mereo Books, an imprint of Memoirs Publishing

The address for Memoirs Publishing Group Limited can be found at www.memoirspublishing.com

The Memoirs Publishing Group Ltd Reg. No. 7834348

The Memoirs Publishing Group supports both The Forest Stewardship Council® (FSC®) and the PEFC® leading international forest-certification organisations. Our books carrying both the FSC label and the PEFC® and are printed on FSC®-certified paper. FSC® is the only forest-certification scheme supported by the leading environmental organisations including Greenpeace. Our paper procurement policy can be found at www.memoirspublishing.com/environment

Typeset in 12/18pt Century Schoolbook
by Wiltshire Associates Publisher Services Ltd. Printed and bound in Great Britain by Printondemand-Worldwide, Peterborough PE2 6XD

In memory of Tony Wright,
great friend and fine piscator

AUTHOR'S ACKNOWLEDGEMENTS

I'd like to give grateful thanks to my wife for having faith, to Steve Barrett for telling me I could do it, to the many anglers with whom I've fished for over 45 years, and to editor Chris Newton for knocking it into shape (rather him than me).

CONTENTS

Chapter 1	A Trout Fishing Paradise	P.1
Chapter 2	Opening Day	P.8
Chapter 3	The Merry Month of May	P.17
Chapter 4	Early Summer	P.25
Chapter 5	Midsummer Madness	P.33
Chapter 6	Taking Stock	P.41
Chapter 7	Late Summer	P.49
Chapter 8	Golden October	P.56
Chapter 9	Codwalloping	P.65
Chapter 10	The Holly and the Ivy	P.74
Chapter 11	In with the New	P.82
Chapter 12	A Poacher, and a Duel	P.91
Chapter 13	The Ides of March	P.100
Chapter 14	A Cross to Bear	P.110
Chapter 15	In Memoriam	P.119
Chapter 16	Fishing in Lilliput	P.128
Chapter 17	The Spring Fair	P.136
Chapter 18	The Threat	P.144
Chapter 19	Taking the Lead	P.152
Chapter 20	Poor Relations	P.161
Chapter 21	Working Party	P.170
Chapter 22	Last Day of the Season	P.178
Chapter 23	Autumn Leaves	P.185
Chapter 24	Healing Hands	P.193
Chapter 25	Winter Draws On	P.201
Chapter 26	A Winter's Tale	P.209
	Epilogue	P.217

CHAPTER ONE

A Trout Fishing Paradise

Star Lake was created by man and perfected by God. It began its life when man scooped thousands upon thousands of tons of gravel and sand out of a quiet water meadow deep in the heart of the Midlands, where the mighty Trent holds sway over the many acres through which it lazily flows in ever-deepening bends before ending its mysterious journey at the sea. This hunger of man's for aggregate for both houses and highways had left this most pleasant of valleys literally littered with hundreds of gravel pits of all shapes and sizes, depths and acidities.

It was now that God took a hand. The depth to which man dug for his myriad pebbles was far below that of the natural water table. There was but one fate in store for the abandoned workings. They steadily filled with water.

Now Piscator is well aware that every puddle that survives even for a few days will acquire an insect population, and Star Lake is no different, for this year she is 60 years old. With a pH reading slightly on the acid side, she now boasts a veritable banqueting hall for those most beloved of fish *Salmo trutta* and *Oncorhynchus mykiss*, the brown trout and the rainbow trout.

You may be wondering at this point why I am providing such an intimate insight into the lake. My reason is that it is the most magnificent of all the waters which it has been my privilege and pleasure to fish. Normally I would scarce mention our lovely little water to anyone, save another honourable piscator, for fear of immediate invasion by poachers, or that most infamous scoundrel the day-ticket man. However, my wife, that most vile of all women known to me, decreed that I must. She was no longer prepared to read of aristocratic waters such as Blagdon, Chew and the like whilst little waters such as ours remained anonymous and unheralded in the angling journals.

I dared to reply that this was the way both I and

my fellow angling acquaintances wished it to remain. Balling her huge right hand instantly into a grotesquely knotted fist, she waved it under my nose and bade me repair at once to the shed and begin scribbling. Dejectedly, I slunk out of the cottage, plodded dolefully down the pretty garden path and quietly letting myself into my sanctum. With shaking hands I struck a vesta, and soon the storm lamp was roaring, filling this chapel to fly fishing with a cheery warm glow which was reflected back time and again from age-old varnish lovingly applied and reapplied down over the years to rods that now stood silent sentinel, safely in their racks on the walls, against the time when we would again sally forth together to conquer the denizens of Star Lake.

That wonderful, heady feeling of peace and tranquillity known to all piscators when in the presence of the fishing deity filled my soul as my eyes went from the rods to the reels, thence to the books and again to the mounted fish which stared for all eternity glassy-eyed into space. Lowering myself into the ancient leather armchair, I inhaled a heady cocktail of aromas that almost defied individual interpretation. The faint, earthy scent of the tackle bag, the newly-proofed wader and the damp of the never-fully-dry net, never forgetting that poignant mildew fragrance from the oft-turned page of some ancient angling tome or catalogue from between the wars from Messrs Hardy, Ogden or Warrington, all combined in a bouquet designed to sooth my fevered brow. I knew then that no matter what suffering that foul and fearsome woman might bring to bear upon my person, I would always have within this shrine the power to cast off her demons.

Presently from without there came a gentle rapping upon the shed door. I recognised the knock at once, and throwing open the portal revealed that leering, shabbily-dressed, slack of mouth, odious reprobate known far and wide as Mortimer Sykes. He was better known to me as the foremost fly fisher within our syndicate, and my dearest friend.

Physical description of this degenerate is difficult. He is unprincipled and unscrupulous, outrageous and shameless, whereas I am decent, moral, good and wise. Strangely, the ladies of the club seem to find him acceptable enough, and odder still, some even find him manly and virile. But, let it be recorded, there has never been a fly fisher like him and year on year, his rod average in both weight and numbers has never been bettered. Hugging his revolting carcase to me, I pulled him in and bade him be seated, all the while beaming at his repugnant face, for after my wife's appalling treatment Mort was just the tonic to fortify me.

He bade me stop grinning at him and to make with the drinks, and I chose my usual five-year elderberry wine, while he partook of his favoured parsnip spirit laced with dry fly floatant. Not so strange when only six months previously it would have been benzene, neat, from his hip flask.

As we sat sipping our beverages and basking in the cosy heat emanating from the paraffin heater, I confided to Mort that which my wife had bade me do. That is, to give literary vent concerning the excellent sport we enjoyed down at Star Lake. True to his piscatorial nature, Mort was deeply affected by this proposed degeneration of the sacred, secret status of the lake. A single tear meandered slowly down his ugly visage, to match the dewy one hanging from his hawk-like nose. Silently he wiped both onto the back of his filthy mitten and rummaged through his pockets, finally producing a hoary old briar, which he proceeded to fill with the most potent and revolting shag. Rasping a match into flame on the stubble under his chin, he quickly had the ancient pipe roaring like an elderly asthmatic blast furnace. The shed quickly filled with acrid fumes which had us both in tears within seconds.

Finally Mort delivered his verdict. It was as brilliant as it was simple. Although he might act the imbecile and look the dullard, he crafted most of the rules of the club, and he now proposed that we invoke Rule Four. In a nutshell, this refers to any action by any member that could affect the quality of the fishing and states that such action must first be discussed by the full membership at an extraordinary meeting. This meant, in all conscience, that I must arrange such a meeting, as I knew in my heart of hearts that once the wider angling fraternity became aware of the joyous opportunities open to piscators at the lake, its peace would be shattered for eternity.

The evening of the meeting had arrived, and as I cast my gaze over the assembled throng of members, I felt nothing save trepidation. Our combined membership is eighty permits: sixty-five men and fifteen women. My monstrous wife, of course, could count on all the women's votes, as none of them would ever countenance gainsaying her, such was the force of her evil personality. I also knew that she would get many of the male votes, as a fair number of them, to their discredit, find her sinewy calves and muscular forearms unduly attractive. Added to that, it had reached my ears that some members mistakenly believed that they would enjoy some sort of kudos should our little water be put upon the piscatorial map, as it were. In addition, it did nothing for my cause that she insisted on parading in front of the assembly on the makeshift podium malevolently swinging her priest, cast at home in bronze and depicting the infant Samuel at prayer, at anyone who seemed to take an interest in my address.

After the polite applause following my speech had abated, my wife took the stage. What followed still leaves me shocked and sickened. Her speech for publicising Star Lake was delivered with all the fury and passion one associates with a certain Herr Hitler addressing the Nuremberg rallies. I should know, as she has the entire collection, faithfully recorded on vinyl, and often listens to them with rapt attention whilst tying flies in the bath. Needless to say, she carried the day, and all the anglers, save Mort and myself, urged me to carry the news, gossip and tales of our fellowship down at the lake to the world.

More than that, it was insisted, by way of a unanimous vote, that I should be the scribe of our piscatorial alliance in perpetuity, or until I meet my maker. My loathsome spouse could, no doubt, have this arranged, so I will continue to report at regular intervals.

Vigilate hoc spatio (watch this space)

CHAPTER TWO

Opening Day

Fishing commences at Star Lake on the first of April. For weeks, the general pressure, strain and stress had been steadily rising among the members until by the eve of the actual day, the excitement could be felt as though it had become a tangible entity.

The reed beds and banks had all been trimmed. The trees that had been starting to interfere with casting last season had been pollarded, and the heavy gates that hid the wooden lodge from prying eyes had been freshly protected with creosote. No small amount of the said substance had mysteriously disappeared, and it was held that Mort had used fractional distillation in order to remove his beloved benzene.

The sun was warm, yet there was a chill wind, and though we knew the rains of winter had departed, spring was yet to fully take root. The loveliest of the trees were already garbed in green, yet possibly the greatest lift came from seeing the young lambs gambolling around their dams in the fields approaching the lake.

In the Audley household, there was only one topic of conversation – how would we fare with tomorrow's opening of the glorious season? My wife, that obnoxious harpy, had in her foetid imagination already won, opened and swallowed the champagne presented for the heaviest bag of the day, and I could hear her discordant mewling as she sang an unpleasant ditty whilst applying a final protective coat of varnish to her nine-foot Hardy's nymph rod. I would happily fish it with a seven line, but with the musculature of her arms and shoulders, she can lay a six out beautifully. Shrew that she may be, she does cast exquisitely.

Her loyal hound, Seyton, bared his fangs as I crept into the green oak conservatory where she keeps her tackle, ties her flies, and generally holds court with her unpleasant cronies. He is an ill-natured cur, with a coat as black as a starless night and eyes like burning coals, but he is faithful unto death and would try to kill me should I offer harm to his mistress.

On this morning however, I entertained no thoughts as to how I could rid myself of the hag, for I was merely dropping off a parcel lately delivered by the dilatory postman Todd.

Normally I would be nervous, as the dog appeared to be in a foul humour, but the package was from Veniard's, and anything from that piscatorial emporium was surely worth running the canine gauntlet.

With an imperious nod of her grotesque head she bade me unwrap the parcel, and with trembling fingers I released a cornucopia of fur and feathers, from guinea fowl to jungle cock and from teal to toucan, along with the traditional hare's mask and multi-coloured seal's fur, the tools of this seductress's trade. With bowed head I stumbled away, knowing I was followed by her triumphant leer, as I could never hope to match her peerless talent in the art of tying flies. Fleeing her seat of power. I sought the sanctuary of my shed to plot and plan, scheme and connive, to wrest the champagne from her grasp on the morrow. My only hope was that I had drawn the premier peg, as one has to fish stationary, keeping to the same peg throughout, due to the attendance of every member on the day.

An hour later, Mort barrelled through the door, turned and kicked it shut. He collapsed into the chair gasping for air, sweat pouring down his hideous countenance. Succumbing to a paroxysm of coughing, he gathered an enormous abundance of phlegm into his mouth before projecting it in the direction of the wood burner in the corner. Luckily, the door of the burner was open, as I had only recently applied the taper to kindling. Once it had been shut, and an hour of hard labour with an abrasive cream and scourer had ensued.

At this juncture I noticed a grisly bundle in each of his filthy hands, and the dangling necks of a brace of pheasants gave mute confirmation as to the nature of their demise. With a shudder, Mort told me that capture had been only narrowly averted – he is a poacher of some reknown, as was his father, who was the last villain in the parish to be taken in a man-trap before their outlawing in 1826. With a shrug, an evil grin and a wink, he proposed that we should eat the evidence, and in no short time, the birds were plucked and in the roasting box atop the stove, with a side tin of fresh thyme, rosemary and sage stuffing to complement the meat.

Mort discharged a soft belch and counted himself full. I had told him of my predicament with regard to the opening day prize, and he now sat in silent contemplation with eyes lidded, softly sucking one of his remaining yellowed teeth. Occasional grunts or sighs would denote an idea being either rejected or stored for further consideration, until with a shout he erupted out of the chair and was through the door with the shout that all would be well on the morrow, as the incumbent, albeit temporarily, of the best peg on the lake would triumph.

Opening morning dawned cold and drizzly, the product of a deep area of low pressure over the Irish Sea. The witch sat opposite me at breakfast, snorting and chortling over some whimsy in the *Angling Times* whilst consuming huge quantities of grilled kidneys, washed down with copious amounts of fresh coffee from a cafetière of burnished silver which carried her family motto, *qui audet adipiscitur* (who dares wins). I could eat nothing as I thought of the disaster that awaited at the lake. Going through tried and tested combinations of Teal, Blue and Silver, Zulu, an Invicta or a safer amalgam of Pheasant Tail, Black & Peacock Spider and any of the buzzers brought me no respite from worry, whereas this fetid spouse of mine left the table with a whispered remark that she would fish the Greenwell's Glory and none other.

Seyton padded behind, turned and showed his teeth. Its creator, Canon Greenwell, would rest uneasy if he knew his fly was going to adorn her cast.

Mort and I climbed into my 1929 four-and-a-half-litre Bentley and left for the lake at eight. My wife immediately roared past in her trusty Land Rover, showering us with gravel, a timely reminder that we must be on our mettle to win our endeavour. We lurched drunkenly down the little-used lanes and byways, arriving jarred and dusty, but well in time for the nine o'clock commencement, to be signalled by the Brigadier's lusty two-pound cannon. Although the drizzle had ceased, there remained a chill breeze from the north-east. Everyone fervently hoped that this year he would charge the ordnance with a blank round rather than the sinister canister used previously, for the shell had reduced Farmer Wright's best tup to a pink mist the previous year and emotions still ran high between the pair. However, no such slaughter was to occur, and with a muted roar and belch from the ancient field piece, the day began in earnest.

First blood went to the Wing Commander after only a few minutes, fishing off the centre platform of the railway bank. This was the windward shore, and with the north-easterly coming on, it would have held slightly cooler water. The killing fly was confirmed a few minutes later as a bloodworm pattern, fished very deep.

My wife, that ghastly Amazonian, was in the top corner of my bank, the sheep bank, with a light, cold wind now almost straight into our faces, for over the course of the morning it had completely changed. Even at a distance, the muscles on her forearms and shoulders stood out, bulging and corded, as she effortlessly punched out the line time and again, careless of the temperature, her upper torso clad only in an ex-army tank top. This picture of sinew and brawn sickened and aroused me in equal measure as I patiently continued a figure-of-eight retrieve of my size seven intermediate line.

I spun, startled, at the sound of someone whispering in my ear, and marvelled yet again at Mort's ability to move silently and almost invisibly. He grinned wickedly, and I gasped as I caught the full import of his words. His report on the catches around the lake was not encouraging, with the Wing Commander leading with a brace. At this half-way point, midday, many were the blanks, with an equal number, like Mort, on just one fish. With a twinkle in his eye, he reported my wife to be fishless, although I have noticed that whenever her name is invoked, he assumes a faraway look, tinged with regret.

With a shudder and a shake of his rounded shoulders, he was soon back, and leaned in close to speak softly into my ear. I staggered and gagged as again the stench of his rotting breath smote my senses, and it was all I could do not to pass out. He told me to fish a Coachman, that beautiful little wet fly with its wings of white goose and fat body of peacock herl, finished off with a light hackle of natural red cock or hen, so suggestive of something alive and very edible. With that, he was off, like an extremely pungent ghost at cock-crow, and as I take good advice from any source, I hastily changed flies. There is an adage that to change one's fly is to change one's luck, and this was surely the case now, for no sooner had the line sunk than I tightened into my first fish, and in less than a minute had wet both my net and my bag.

I sat down to enjoy a Marmite sandwich and a nip from the flask, but was soon up again, eager to discover if I could replicate my earlier success, and sure enough after half a dozen casts I was rewarded with that thrilling tug signalling another fish on.

I caught the prescribed two brace easily enough and returned another three fish before the Brigadier's cannon loudly brought proceedings to a close. My closest rival with three trout, but short on weight, was the Wing Commander, who graciously presented me with a rehoboam of champagne, six bottles' worth, an ample quantity for a night's consumption with Mort.

I watched the harridan leave, Seyton malevolently staring at me through the Land Rover's rear window, until I was unable to distinguish between his eyes and the rear lights of the vehicle. Late I saw Mort near the deserted lodge, rinsing out a bait box in the old outdoor Belfast sink. He raised his shoulders, winked, melted into the dark trees, and was gone. I felt a chill in the pit of my stomach. I approached and looked into the sink in time to see a maggot disappear into the plughole. I shuddered as the enormity of his crime sank in; he had baited my fishing spot in order for me to triumph! Trembling with anger, I slipped the larger of my priests into my hand and went in search of the wretch.

CHAPTER THREE

The Merry Month of May

I cursed loud and long as again I failed to complete the parachute hackle on my pathetic attempt at a Mayfly variation. This is arguably the most effective dry fly ever invented. The reason it works so well is that the parachute hackle allows the fly to sit flush to the water, making it look more realistic to the fish and thereby inducing takes.

A mocking, sardonic chuckle echoed from the doorway of my shed, and startled, I spun round in my old captain's chair to gape at the bovine appearance of my dear wife. Clad in a revealing camouflage-coloured boiler suit, she epitomized all that is foul yet feminine. Moving to my tying vice remarkable quickly in her high-leg dispatch riders' boots, she swiftly righted the hackle, finished the fly and held it up to the light for inspection. The size fourteen fly looked incredibly delicate in her stubby, grime lined fingers, reflecting a myriad points of light, and I marvelled once again at the disparity between the grace of her flies and the inelegance of her persona.

Grabbing hold of my collar, she lifted me out of the chair and hurled me towards the door, where I came to a stop as my I thudded painfully into the jamb. Groping above, I grasped the telescopic fish tailer, inscribed with the motto *Absit Inuria* (let injury be absent), from above the lintel and snapped into a menacing on-guard position, oblivious to the daemonhound Seyton sitting directly outside. He immediately sank his fangs into my calf, and I lost consciousness as my brutish bride brought down a solid brass marrow spoon viciously against my temple.

Awareness returned slowly to the pungent aroma of fly floatant wafting under my nose as my wife narrowed her eyes and pronounced me fit. She had entered my sanctum, without appointment it seemed, in excited response to a missive she had received via our lax and indolent postman, Todd. The unprovoked attack on myself was mere exuberance on her part, whilst Seyton had barely marked my leg, as she had instructed him simply to deter me and not maim. The cur had an extensive understanding of vocabulary, and I shuddered as I realised that most of it concerned the delivery of pain.

In tones that jarred the nerves, she told me of the contents of the letter, leaving me numb with shock and not a little despair. By no doubt nefarious means, she had managed to lure the Editor in Chief of *The Piscatorial Gazette*, Sir Donald Edward, into coming to Star Lake, with a view to including it in his monthly review of the foremost trout waters in England and Wales, should he judge it to meet that august organ's impeccable standards. I had met the man but once and had found him tolerably sufficient as a fishing writer, but realised now that he was an absolute shower.

The woman I feared most then instructed me to inform all members, *tout de suite,* of the forthcoming visit of this sewer masquerading as a journalist, and to make sure his sojourn amongst us be memorable. Immediately I went in search of Mort. I had left him servicing the Bentley, with strict instructions to rinse out the supercharger with alcohol, but found him intoxicated and sprawled across the seats, an empty bottle of methylated spirits clutched lovingly to his chest. Unable to contain myself, I carried him across the gravel drive and catapulted him into the ornamental fishpond. With muttered apologies to the resident common carp – I will not tolerate the gaudy ostentation of the Koi – I held him out of the water and vigorously slapped both cheeks. He sobered remarkably quickly, even attempting a sly head butt, until he realised with whom he was dealing.

I allowed but two minutes of his grovelling before propelling him into the Bentley and thence to the lodge down at the lake, where we had to convene a council of war. The supercharged engine whined lustily as we hurtled down ancient, dusty byways at eighty miles per hour, and I wondered miserably how we were to avert the worst carnage ever seen at the lake since a member, who will remain anonymous, dared to raise the issue of day tickets.

There were four fellow piscators plying their trade at the lake, thereby making the required quorum for an emergency meeting: the Brigadier, Farmer Wright, the Reverend Farthing, Miss Arkwright, and of course Mort and I. By midnight, we had reached agreement on a strongly-worded letter to all members advising them to boycott the visit of Sir Donald, thereby illustrating to this insufferable bounder the feelings of the membership that his visit was neither wanted nor warranted.

Mort slept for the last two hours with his head on the table. Finally he raised one bleary, bloodshot eye and asked if we were done. He declared us fools and said that even as we spoke, the harlot at my house would be actively seducing Sir Donald, and that he would be hers forever – if not by now, then by dawn's early chorus. With heads hung in shame, we endured the rebuke, fully aware that he was right, and were reduced to tears as he went around the table, absolving us individually from our collective folly and assuring all would be well as long as matters were left to him. With eyes wetly shining did we regard this malodorous runt who stood foursquare before us, ready aye ready to do battle in our cause. The moment soured somewhat upon leaving, as the spinster Arkwright pressed her door key into Mort's calloused palm with a whispered plea for haste.

The arrival of Sir Donald at Star Lake was as impressive as it was dramatic, as we witnessed his approach down the long dusty track that serves as entry to this delightful water. The Hispano-Suiza he drove, at just under seven litres engine displacement, was the finest motorcar in the world, and I felt myself briefly warm towards the man, until with a start, I remembered the premise of his visit. I mentally composed myself to be civil but cool to this basely-born mongrel of the angling press.

With a flourish, he opened the passenger door to allow my wife egress from that magnificent vehicle, and whilst she entertained the onlooking members with glimpses of her long, shapely, sinuous legs, freshly shaved and lightly sprinkled with balsam, he proceeded to unload his tackle from the car. There was an audible gasp from the assembly, for never before had such tackle graced our little haven. The finest rods, reels and lines were spread on a purple velvet blanket as he informed us of his intention to perform a small demonstration of casting prowess. A strange silence settled, and my heart leapt as I realised he had committed the vilest faux-pas by having the effrontery to exhibit himself in this fashion.

The backhand, reach, tuck, sidearm and roll casts were meticulously performed to a stony silence, but then he faltered on the haul as too late he realised that an Englishman should never attempt to stand over and above his fellows. For this brutish behaviour alone, he was marked as a cad.

He had but one chance at redemption, for to prove himself as a true piscator he would have to make us overlook his former beastly behaviour, and well he knew this, for he announced his intention to fish clad only in a camouflaged loincloth, using a pheasant tail nymph on an ungreased cast – a feat to be performed only by the extremely devout. Before commencing, he wished to make use of certain facilities, and my wife naturally conducted him to the newly-installed Coxley-Shaw mobile water closet. This was the latest in ambulatory conveniences, and the manufacturer's soubriquet for this wondrously peripatetic commode was the Thunderbox. No sooner had his ignoble behind touched the highly-polished mahogany seat than the contraption moved, slowly at first, but gathering pace as the slight incline toward the lake took effect. Cries of shock rent the air as the appliance splashed mightily into the water, turning to outrage as the assemblage observed Sir Donald clambering groggily out of the lake without the loincloth, but still sporting a gentleman's reinforced abdominal support. Never had the club been so disrespected, as he had led all to believe that his double-haul casting was produced without enhancement of his physique. As a result, as he fled the scene of his utter embarrassment, he was mocked and jeered by all until the Hispano was a speck in the distance.

Even my consort looked disconcerted as she realised that another of her schemes had been thwarted. She flashed an evil look at me and I realised for one sickening moment that she thought me responsible for the debacle, but then her meaty brow again furrowed into rest and I knew I was safe from her revenge for the time being. I managed a timid wave as she rattled off homeward in the elderly Land Rover.

Mort joined me as I went through my pockets looking for the key that secures the lodge gates, and we shared a companionable pipe whilst reviewing the events of the day. I was spent after the angst, dread and apprehension of Sir Donald's visit, whereas Mort was strangely ebullient. He nodded and pressed something cold and metallic into my hand before turning and disappearing wraith-like into the night. Without looking, I knew the locking pin for the brake on the Thunderbox nestled in my hand.

CHAPTER FOUR

Early Summer

On the lake, summer begins in the first week of June. The swifts and swallows are back from the tropics, wildly cavorting across the sky as they fill their beaks and bellies, ready to feed their chicks as they raise another brood. It can also be a time of fluctuating fortunes for the piscator, from easily bagging a two-brace limit on a slowly-fished Black and Peacock Spider to blanking the very next day after exhausting the contents of the fly wallet.

Mort and I were experiencing one of the latter days as the sun shone fiercely down from a cloudless azure sky. A light south-westerly breeze was creating a lop on the water that would nicely hide our antics from the trout, but both bags and nets stayed resolutely dry, whilst old hands around the water were convinced a further stocking was needed.

I temporarily ceased swapping flies and glanced across at him as he lay intermittently nipping from a hip flask of benzene and sucking at a rustic old briar heaped with smouldering odious shag, flue dried for extra punch. I marvelled, not for the first time, at his ugliness, his unseemly manners and unsightly carcass.

The Moriarty sisters approached and we shared gossip about our lack of success with the trout. Mort leered incessantly at the delightful pair until they left red-faced and embarrassed, although he insisted that they were invigorated and possibly in heat. I could stand this coarse and impolite behaviour no longer and immediately set about his rough and unpolished frame with a small lash I keep about my person, soon bringing the uncouth wretch to heel.

Soon after, we departed, having blanked. A quick check of the returns book revealed that the few trout that had been caught had been taken first thing on the windward sheep bank. We swore to return later to see what the evening rise would bring, and the inscription above the lodge door continued to echo that very thought:

Numquam cede (never give up)

On arriving home after a hectic dash back in the Bentley, we found that shrew to which I was wed disporting herself in a hammock in the cottage garden, resplendent in a knitted wool swimsuit and wellingtons. The evil cur Seyton lay within easy call of his mistress should painful retribution for some perceived slight or insult be necessary or required. I thought she looked attractive and vivacious, whereas Mort decided actions speak louder than words and broke wind lustily and with gusto over the unfortunate hound, who tried to stand, but collapsed wretchedly into a stupor. Evil, angry lights danced in her eyes as she glared like a basilisk at Mort, yet he stood his ground under that terrible onslaught and I again sensed some message pass between them, undecipherable to me.

Finally the luckless canine regained enough of its wits to stagger uncertainly back into our large and handsome cottage, leaving the three of us in a mute tableau, finally broken by the harridan in my life as she spoke of an idea that had formed in her calculating brain. Her latest flash of inspiration to put the lake on the piscatorial map was to purchase a monstrous trout of some fourteen pounds, well in excess of the rod-caught record, introduce it to Star Lake and have one of the ladies at the club catch it to instant national acclaim, thereby catapulting our little water well and truly into the limelight. The crone was nothing if not persistent, claiming that the story of a female captor would capture the public's imagination and certainly put our charming, attractive water into the headlines.

I needed all my self-discipline to prevent myself smiting the witch hip and thigh, as I reasoned she could not be aware of the harm to both village and lake that would arise from this sensational publicity. The Englishman needs to remain anonymous both in his home and playground.

Mort caught my eye, raised one bushy, unkempt brow, and gave me a look. It was all I needed to quickly follow him down the garden path to the shed. Once inside, he kicked the door shut with one flick of his monstrous steel toe-capped boot and let forth a stream of invective seldom heard outside a dockside dive, unless one should include that which is heard occasionally at home when that cantankerous ogress loses the pot of Hammerite with which she adorns her nails.

I was at a loss as to why Mort should be so affected, and having seated and calmed him, I put the taper to the primus and made a pot of his favourite Orange Pekoe tea. In his faltering, awkward, graceless fashion, he recounted why the peace, serenity and beauty of the lake, and to a lesser extent that of the village, should not be subjected to the modern, crass and ungenteel tenets of this twentieth century life, and stated that my wife's lust for recognition of any kind was a direct threat to all he held dear. On that note, he bade me leave him to it, and a finger of ice traced a path down my spine, for as I looked into his strange, simian eyes, I detected a resolve that few would or should dare to confront.

The gorgon of the cottage had me broadcast the announcement of the introduction of the enormous trout into Star Lake the following week as soon as possible, and much to Mort's and my surprise, it was counted an excellent plan by the majority of the club members. He was all for visiting violence upon the more outspoken, until, trapping his thumb agonisingly tightly in the fly vice, I convinced him of the folly of such an action.

The day scheduled for the release of the leviathan dawned bright, blue and calm, with a near full turnout of the membership. To mark the day, the Moriarty sisters had been coerced into providing the kind of lavish spread for which they had gained some fame, and laid the foundations of a thriving catering business. Today's fare was to be a cold collation with a centrepiece of a freshly-barbecued prime sea trout, and I for one could hardly wait for teatime.

A dilapidated little flatbed truck hove into view as it approached the lodge gates, with a decaying, neglected, galvanised tank secured to its rear. A scruffy, seedy-looking man in a rakishly-tilted bowler hat alighted from the decrepit vehicle and raised his chin in the direction of the Brigadier. Several of the members instantly adopted menacing stances, and Bayleaf, the vicar's gardener, covertly released the blade of his swordstick. I feared for the hatchery man's safety, and in order to allow him to leave the lake without harm to his person, I stepped in and quickly stunned him with my priest. Mort nodded in approbation and dragged the unconscious lout to the cab of his ramshackle vehicle, unceremoniously bundling him behind the wheel. He then vaulted to the tank, and dipping hands therein, produced the recently purchased behemoth.

She was very large, but tatty of fin and thin of flank and obviously an ageing brood hen. My lip curled as I looked back towards the wagon and made as if to approach the blackguard, who had recovered from my swipe and was engaged in starting the engine. With a wild look, he crashed the wreck into gear and was gone in a haze of blue smoke.

Mort gently carried the piscean colossus to the small bay where the two rowboats were tied up and slipped her into the green depths. She would not venture far, as he had suspended a net across the mouth of the inlet, thereby making her swift capture an inevitability the following week. The sex of the captor would be equally inevitable, for the bay was to be ladies only until the freakish fish was seen again.

The meal was a success, with the Moriarty sisters cementing their reputation as caterers to the elite. Especially toothsome was the sea trout, barbecued to perfection under the ministrations of Mort, who served the fish headless and tailless with the skin and fins replaced by alternate slices of cucumber and gherkin, complemented by a strong lime *jus*.

After all had departed, triumphantly led by the beldam that shares my bed, Mort and I sat in companionable silence staring over the lake. The early evening was windless, and the trout were noisily sipping spent spinners and emerging imagos from the placid surface. I was however in no mood to pick up the rod as I contemplated the ramifications when one of the ladies landed the whale. I remarked that despite her age and condition, she remained a trout of note, and Mort agreed, especially, he said, as we had all just eaten her.

I looked askance, and then grinned broadly. Mort nodded, winked and was gone.

CHAPTER FIVE

Midsummer Madness

Named by the Roman Senate in honour of Caesar, July is on average the warmest month of the year, and trawling through previous logs, I saw that it was second in difficulty for luring trout to that of August. The sun beat mercilessly down out of a clear blue sky, and for the umpteenth time I cursed myself for not limiting my fishing at this time of the year to the start and end of the day.

Mort's face was the colour of beetroot as he repeatedly punched out his weight-forward floating line carrying a large bushy dry fly of indeterminate origin and material towards the centre of Star Lake, as we had espied the odd riser cruising atop the very deep water in the middle. The fly was based loosely on the Tup's Indispensable pattern, and Mort had tried to avail himself of the prescribed washed wool from the scrotum of a ram. His release from the psychiatric ward had coincided with his physical recovery, but to this day he will not cross the sheep field if Farmer Wright's favoured ovine Casanova is amongst the ewes.

At one of the clock, with no trout forthcoming, we recorded the blanks at the lodge and then wearily turned the Bentley towards home, rest and refreshment. Rattling along the dusty lanes at a gentle forty, the four-and-a-half litre engine barely ticking over, we observed a commotion upon the road ahead. Cowie, the swineherd, was struggling with an enormous sow he was trying to transfer from his cart and into the field which held the farrowing sheds. This porcine monster, which bore a passing resemblance to my dear wife, was cunning, shrewd and potentially very dangerous, again not unlike my loving spouse.

Clutching our sides with laughter at this resemblance, we fell out of the car in order to assist Cowie, an unpleasant individual with the reputation of being somewhat of a scoundrel. Certainly a glance into his deep-set malevolent eyes marked him as both a lout and rake. Mort, with no temperament for a gentle approach, grasped the porker's curly tail between both hoary hands and heaved with all the strength his revolting frame could muster. The resultant plaintive squeal from the pig was so heartrending that my previous mirth died on my lips as the hog struggled in vain to release herself from Mort's not so tender embrace. With a cry of triumph, he let go, simultaneously planting a very large hobnailed boot to the animals' quite filthy behind. The swine slowly turned a baleful stare upon Mort and I felt a shiver pass through me as hatred shone from her little eyes and an enmity was forged between the two on that very spot that only further violence would undo. Mort too had felt the naked malice in that gaze, and primitive that he was, knew some little fear grown out of that animosity. Cowie led the unprotesting sow into the field, and true to his low nature, the rascal thanked us not.

In something of a sombre mood, we arrived home and repaired to the large and pretty cottage garden to stow the tackle and cleanse ourselves of honest sweat. The optimum approach was to douse one another with a bucket of cold water, set aside in the shade that very morning before we ventured out. However, unknown to me, Susan, my wife's daily helper, had added a goodly amount of caustic soda to one of the buckets in preparation for scouring the drains. Whereas I had marked her as imbecilic and dense, I now included moronic and obtuse.

When I had doused Mort in a strong metal base solution also known as lye, his clothes began to smoulder, then pain intervened as nerve endings frantically communicated trouble to his somewhat addled brain. With a scream, he launched himself at the mock gothic ornamental pond for the second time that year and his sighs echoed round the stunning courtyard as the corrosive effects of his shower were neutralised.

Trembling with rage, I went in search of retribution against the person of the hapless maid, and found her cowering in an old pine blanket box in the hallway. This coffer was ancient and had been used once upon a time to store my old school uniforms. It was inscribed with that old worthy institutions' motto *suma fide ac probitate* (supreme faith and honesty). Grabbing her wrist, I extracted her corpulent body like a fat winkle from its shell and raised the small lash I always carried against such an event. But then a low menacing growl froze further retaliation. Seyton, that hound from hell, issued another rumble from his massive chest and with due caution, I fled the scene and caught up with Mort, who stood dripping in the driveway, looking like a singed and tatty scarecrow, and roared away in the Bentley to Star Lake, where succour and peace awaited.

After disporting ourselves about the lodge for a couple of hours, once tea and an abundance of sandwiches provided by the Moriarty sisters had replenished the inner man, we felt ready to fish again. I extricated Mort from the side of the spinster Arkwright who was passing the time between angling sessions stretched on a lounger clad in a tiny bikini worshipping the sun. Together we had burgled the lost property cupboard – one day soon the committee must make the effort to find the owner of an upper set of dentures and a glass eye – and Mort was now almost presentable, his burning skin no longer a concern after repeated applications of cold tea and calamine lotion.

We stood on the veranda and surveyed the view towards the railway bank yonder. The sun had not yet set, but was low and mellowing, and the light breeze from the south would not hinder casting should an evening rise occur.

Hardly had the thought crossed my mind before we beheld the start of that very happy circumstance. Should I live to be a hundred, I will never lose that excitement, that tightening of the chest, that incredible expectancy, as one covers a rising fish. In reality, only once in a hundred casts does one connect with the fish, but in theory, every cast can do so. In truth, that is why we do this madness, year on year, from April to October, and we love it.

Mort had observed fish rising opposite beneath the railway bank, probably to insects blown onto the water, and had gone to investigate. Piscator that he is, on the third cast, a fat rainbow trout of some two pounds fell for a slowly-pulled Hare's Ear and we all began to retrieve in order to move round and join him.

However, all activity ceased as a tableau unfolded before us. In his haste to cover the rising fish, Mort had not noticed anything in the field beyond the railway lines and was blissfully unaware that the large pink sow we had encountered earlier was now ambling curiously towards the fence. As recognition flared within the tiny brain of the pig, she released a squeal of fury and rushed the wooden fence encircling the field, determined to bear down on the source of the misery inflicted upon her earlier that day. The fence splintered and parted as nearly two hundred and fifty pounds of pork thundered towards an unsuspecting Mort, who only became aware of his impending doom when the hog let forth a terrible cry, plunging through the hawthorn hedge separating Star Lake from the rail network. Cruel thorns tore at her flesh, but that did not impede her passage as she cleared the hedge, reset her course and flew for her human target, determined to bite, trample and gore until he drew breath no more.

Mort gave a wail of pure terror and raced off down the bank back towards the relative shelter and haven of the lodge, whilst we all watched in rapt horror as the porcine sprinter narrowed the gap between them. We feared the end was nigh for Mort, as did Miss Arkwright, who wept copiously and wetly into her handkerchief, whilst I cursed for a fool the idiot swineherd that had moved the hog to such an insecure enclosure.

The Brigadier watched with the knowing eye of one who has seen action in the trenches and on the broad, dusty veldt. He who had faced danger and lived to become a better man turned and hurried into the lodge, where he produced a large, ornate key and unlocked a long metal cupboard bolted to the wall. From therein, a Boys rifle appeared in his hands. Designed as an anti-tank weapon, it fired a bullet over half an inch in calibre and could penetrate armour up to an inch in thickness, with a muzzle velocity of nearly three thousand feet per minute. The pernicious porker was dead and minus her head long before the smoke had cleared the lodge steps.

We laid the cadaver upon the rude threshold of Cowie's filthy little hovel, as he was the rightful owner, and it lay there all the next day. Word spread of

Cowie's craven departure, and much was made of Bayleaf the gardener's belief that the dastardly, gutless coward had seen the headless corpse as a threat from local gangsters he had no doubt crossed. The pig was turned into sausages, some two hundred pounds of them in all, which were distributed to the needy throughout the parish.

CHAPTER SIX

Taking Stock

With a sigh of satisfaction and a palpable frisson of joy as a sudden passing sensation of excitement shuddered through my frame, I gently laid the ancient fisherman's almanac onto the bedside cabinet beside my antique Belgian folding trigger pocket revolver. Made in Liege, it was a point two-two calibre rimfire weapon, easily capable of disabling the largest of cracksmen, or burglar as they are now commonly known, should either attempt to disturb the sleep of myself or my appalling wife.

The piscatorial forecaster had suggested that

August the sixteenth through to the twenty- fourth was the most auspicious time to sally forth with the rods, and as that was a mere two days hence, I was indeed a happy man.

I lay there beaming and began chuckling as I recalled last month's incident with Mort and the sow at Star lake, and such was my mirth that I laughed and hooted until the bed shook. It was an unwise move and one I immediately regretted, as my wife, drooling from the corner of her offensive maw as she slept, rolled onto her back and began to snore. The snorting and rattling sound made by the vibration of the airway tissue at the back of her mouth, nose and throat during sleep as she breathed in and out reached a volume and resonance which rattled the windows in their frames, and I knew I would get no more sleep that night until she desisted.

Reaching below the bed, my fingers came across the rod-rest I sought and I thrust the business end of the instrument into one of her magnificently meaty buttocks. With a roar she awoke and clutched me by the throat, shaking me as a terrier might a rat, until I lied, telling her I had remembered that tonight was the full moon, and therefore the eventide on which we made love. Rewarding me with a ghastly smile, she pulled me to her foul bosom, and I must draw a veil over what followed. Needless to say, I staggered out of the bedchamber the next morning dishevelled, my nightcap askew and nightshirt in tatters, a look of wonder and awe on my face, and a half-remembered saying in my mind that I should have heeded: *vir sapit qui pauca loquitur (*the wise man says little).

I repaired to the kitchen and discovered Mort deep in conversation with Susan, the lackadaisical daily servant who was supposed to be cooking my breakfast kidneys at that moment. She threw back her head, trilling at some lewd and lascivious comment from Mort, who ran his calloused fingers languidly up and down her hairy forearms. Bringing their heads crisply together, I bade them desist and attend me at once. Mort gave an oath and clenched his fists as he turned, but one glance at my finely-chiselled features and the Fairbairn-Sykes double-edged fighting knife that had magically appeared in my hand from within the folds of my satin night attire dissuaded him from further action, and a swift boot to the rump of Susan in the direction of the Aga produced breakfast in but a short time.

After I had dressed and completed my toilet, Mort and I coaxed the Bentley into life and roared explosively into the lane and thence onto the road that would take us to Fraser's trout farm and hatchery. The main site is located next to the institute for the criminally insane and is fed by the Drover Beck, delivering naturally pure clear water which is sourced from springs in the surrounding hills and limestone rocks.

It was from here, for the first time this season, that we at Star Lake were sourcing our trout. The majority were rainbow trout, but we would take the small, fingerling brown trout to grow on and finally a few mutant fish, or American brook trout, raised under artificial conditions at the hatchery. They were imbued with power and magic, and with a near-legendary fighting strength to test the mettle and breaking strain of the anglers and leaders alike down at the lake.

The level agreed at the AGM was to be 50 fish per acre, so as to make the fishing neither too easy nor too difficult. Seeing the trout swimming around the stew ponds made me feel giddy and Mort positively delirious, so I quickly got him away and with great difficulty decided not to leave him at the asylum next door.

That evening after dinner, as my wife and I sipped a fine cognac in front of a roaring log fire, I mentioned the trip to the trout farm that morning. She ignored me and simply stared into my eyes, a coquettish smile playing on her dry and cracked lips as she breathlessly suggested an early night. The firelight played upon her awful visage, highlighting the onset of a light beard and moustache, and I felt truly sick at the prospect of a repeat of last night. As she saw this the light died in her eyes, replaced by a tightening of her lantern jaw and clenching of her fist as her hellish true nature came to the fore. Seyton, who a moment before had lain fast asleep at his mistress's feet, now stood lightly on his paws, ready to attack should she signal the command.

The tension of the situation was broken by the arrival of Mort, who stumbled in as the lounge door flew back on its hinges to crash against the wall. He was accompanied by a tall, emaciated sketch of a man instantly recognisable as Josiah Hardwick, president of the Sedgebrook Fly-Fishing Club. Hardwick's lugubrious countenance and sad demeanour, at once both saddened and depressed, instilled in all those who encountered him a need for an immediate intake of alcohol or other stimulant. I had not seen this gloomy man since the start of the season and wondered what his pensive presence might betoken. My shrewish wife gave him neither thought nor attention, and without a word she flounced out of the room, followed by her hound, who glared at us balefully, displaying his fangs.

I bade Hardwick sit and tell us the reason for his visit, whilst Mort skilfully prepared for him a powerful cocktail of navy rum and blackcurrant juice. I would not be at ease with him in any way, as our clubs shared an enmity stretching back over the years. Ours was the better club, with superior, more skilful members, fishing premium water for good quality trout. I was however, prepared to be magnanimous and decided to hear him out. Then I would instruct Mort to throw him out.

He launched into a rambling, at times incoherent, account of woe at their club; in a nutshell, they had run out of fish. The next delivery was not due for another month, with the list of blanks growing daily. His anglers were getting restless and had threatened to burn the clubhouse down should conditions not improve at their inferior, humble pond.

My lip curled as I regarded his stooped and sagging demeanour, but my greater intellect demanded I offer him aid and succour, and I agreed to let him have half of the delivery that was due next week. I allowed him to prostrate himself and cringe whilst I looked down upon him with a smirk on my finely-chiselled features and dismissed him with an imperious nod after the required minute of fawning had come to a close. Mort saw him out and returned with an unreadable expression on his ugly visage and breathing hard through his nose. I thought he looked embarrassed, should that be possible for such a shallow cove, but for what reason I could not imagine.

As a rule Mort oversaw the transfer of fish from the

stocking truck to the lake, but on this occasion he personally carried out the operation, forsaking aid either from the members or the fat and jolly little delivery man, who incessantly winked and chortled at anyone who caught his eye. I thought him a half-wit and feeble minded and told Mort so. Again he rewarded me with a grim expression and a slight shake of the head before continuing with the restocking process, clad in his traditional leather apron and dun-coloured breachclout. After which, he was to go with the imbecile to Sedgebrook and stock their squalid little pond with the boon of fish kindly supplied by myself.

The dullard from the trout farm, having completed the job at Star Lake, even had the temerity to stick out his grubby paw for a tip, and I stung it soundly with the swagger stick I keep secreted in my finest calf leather boots. Mort looked appalled and turned away to climb into the jaunty red cab of the truck as I stuck my tongue out at the blockhead, who stood before me sucking his fingers in pain.

Days passed slowly into weeks during that turgid August. Members had taken to muttering under their breath at my approach as the tally of fish taken fell. Able piscators like myself struggled for a single fish, and I felt sedition in the air. I knew fear for the first time when I discovered a box of firelighters left in my front porch. Equally disturbing were the reports from Sedgebrook of fantastic sport, and the suggestion that some of our members might consider changing allegiance. I doubted this, as my heroic leadership over the years had been peerless and I did not think their admiration for me had dimmed in the least.

I sought Mort out, as he had taken to avoiding me, even cutting our weekly fly-tying sessions, to demand he assist in upturning once again the fortunes of our club. I found him sitting on the lodge stairs, quietly whittling a piece of dogwood into a fair representation of the Venus de Milo.

I ordered him to reverse the current decline at our club and received a stinging slap to my face, and another, and another, as he recited a list of transgressions on my part. I started to protest and received a stunning blow to the head as he continued the litany of my misdemeanours to my fellow man and my unchecked rush into caddishness and becoming an all-round bounder. He had stocked us only with the fingerling brown trout and had given all of the rainbows and brook trout to the Sedgebrook club as punishment for my boorish behaviour. Before fading into the trees at the edge of Star Lake, he pointed a trembling, filthy finger at me and bade me change my ways or risk losing our friendship forever.

CHAPTER SEVEN

Late Summer

The last week of August tumbled rapidly into September, and with falling temperatures, the trout of Star Lake began to feed more avidly. With the addition of the last stock of the year, fishing was more or less back to the levels one would expect.

I had not spoken to Mort after his assault and was emotionally still shocked and sore at the ferocity of the attack, but an hour with the Reverend Farthing, who had witnessed the onslaught, had put the business firmly and squarely into context. His perceptive assessment of the situation had rendered me speechless with embarrassment and had elevated Mort to saintliness in my estimation. I had been a boor and a bounder, a stinker and a worm, whereas Mort had selflessly acted to save me from myself. I sent apologies and reparation to all those I had offended, issued an invitation to Hardwick to fish Star Lake, and sent a black pudding and a pickled egg to Fraser for his man at the fish farm. My profound apologies to Mort were welcomed as we three sat in the reverend's study, with two ancient briars and the vicar's acrid cheroot combining to make as thick a fug as was acceptable without one of us being asphyxiated. With tears from the fumes rolling down his cheeks, the dapper little priest kept his parsnip brandy, distilled by Mort's own apparatus, circulating until we all three, with slurring speech and malfunctioning limbs, bade each other a cheery goodnight and headed to bed; Farthing up the stairs, me to the most charming cottage in all the village and Mort to the spinster Arkwright's outhouse, his lodging place of the moment.

September is the month of the big fish, the glass-caser, the specimen hunter's fantasy. It is the time when the portly matrons (for the majority of these leviathans are female) leave their bolt-holes and special, hard-to-reach hiding places and venture out into open water, sipping a prostrate spinner here or gulping a struggling crane fly there, and therefore laying themselves open to capture. Many are the nights I have awoken in a cold sweat in a tangle of bed linen to discover the capture of such a monster had been merely a tangled dream. The reality is then a nightmare, as my frightful wife, realising I am awake, will mew with pleasure and drag me struggling back under the covers to sample her infernal delights.

I picked Mort up the next morning bright and early from Miss Arkwright's neat little terrace, and it did not seem that he had spent the night in the outhouse. From his dissipated appearance and generally exhausted state, I would warrant he had slept little, probably due to his excitement at the prospect of today's fishing. We bundled ourselves merrily into the Bentley and in no time had the supercharged engine screaming as we rattled down the thoroughfares, lanes and byways at a dangerous sixty miles an hour, intent on arriving at Star Lake in short order. Both of us were eager to catch a large fish, as we remembered during the conversation on the way that a certain promise had been made to our urbane and witty cleric the night before when in our cups which involved a votive offering for the Harvest Thanksgiving ceremony later this month. This worldwide and very ancient custom is celebrated in Britain, where we have given thanks for successful harvests since pagan times by singing, praying and decorating our churches with baskets of fruit and food in a festival known as The Harvest Festival.

We groaned simultaneously, as all piscators are aware that to promise a fish is to lose a fish, and we agreed to angle with the utmost seriousness and intent until a sizeable specimen was captured to grace the padre's harvest table.

Four days later, we were still active in our quest. My tennis elbow had returned due to continuous casting and Mort lying prostrate in a state of collapse on the bank. Things were reaching a critical point, the rector having asked us pointedly last eve whether or not an offering would be forthcoming for the occasion of the festival on the morrow. Many fish had come to the net, with none in excess of a mere two pounds. This brought to mind the well-known maxim *'cave quid dicis, quando, et cui'* (be careful what you say and to whom you say it).

I prodded Mort with my toe as pain lanced up my arm in response to the overuse of certain muscles, but Mort continued to lie on his back with a beatific smile on his face as he gently slept, his craggy features at rest in a pleasant mask, due in no small degree to a libation taken during lunch. For a moment I forgot about the pious Farthing and our bothersome promise, but then I espied that very friar hurrying round the bank towards us.

Mort stirred extremely rapidly as I rammed my rod tip up his red and heavily-veined nose and stood rapidly to attention as the prelate stopped before us. He told us that one of his oldest parishioners, Walter Edison, was nearly ready to meet his maker and therefore required his presence, and asked us to place the fish directly in the church. He presented me with an ornate old key, gave a quick benediction and was gone.

I looked at Mort and sighed. He looked at me and grinned, then held out his hand for the key and bade me go home as all would be well. Having heard those words so many times before, I was at once relieved for myself, but disturbed and on edge, for someone always paid a price of sorts when things were left to Mort.

That night I lay abed unable to sleep, not because of the rasping, snorting harpy next to me but for worrying over Mort, who at that moment would be abroad in the night performing felonies and the like on my behalf. I cursed myself for being craven.

The sighing of the wind outside and the cracking of old wainscots as the old house settled usually calmed me, but on this night it filled me with foreboding and apprehension, and my heart was in my mouth as I heard the soft footfall outside the bedroom door and watched in sick fascination as the ornate brass handle began to rotate. With a scream I leapt out of bed, grabbed the pikestaff attached to the suit of armour in the corner and rushed to the door, to be confronted by a shivering semi-coherent Mort. He stood trembling in his dripping combination underwear, his mouth opening and closing in an unholy accompaniment to the water falling from his long johns.

We repaired to the kitchen, where a remarkable sight met my eyes. A large cock brown trout weighing probably in excess of ten pounds lay on the table, an enormous kype and a pronounced curvature of the jaws confirming its sex. I could only look from the fish to Mort and back again and wonder what miracle he had yet again performed to pull this particular piece of fat out of the fire, but I stopped abruptly as I spotted the ventilated aluminium bait box clasped loosely in his calloused hands. I gently pried the container from him and lifted the lid to see several large lobworms writhing and scouring themselves in the moss. They had been placed in the tin to toughen their skins so as to remain longer on the hook.

Mort had committed the ultimate sin; he had angled for a non-migratory trout with bait. He looked to me for understanding, but I turned my head away as I failed to comprehend this most dreadful of crimes.

I then did the only thing I could, which was to phone the vicarage. The Reverend Farthing arrived promptly and without fuss, bringing with him his accoutrements of absolution, and throughout the night he performed the piscatorial rituals of cleansing and atonement, beginning with the burning of the sinner's clothes and the removal of all body hair. This presented perhaps the greatest obstacle, as Mort was covered in what one could only call a pelt, but this intelligent man of the cloth burned the worst tufts off with a lighted taper, with only small whimpers issuing from Mort. The fishing rod used to capture the fish was then ceremonially snapped across the penitent's head and the pieces burnt, along with the line, in a crucible. The resultant ash was then mixed with a little wine and imbibed, in sure recognition that a crime had been committed but that the criminal accepted the burden of guilt and responsibility.

At the end of the purification process, the holy man confirmed all was forgiven and that when the good lord called Mort into his divine landing net, he would be judged good enough to keep. The only thing that had saved Mort was that he had taken the fish for the greater glory of the Harvest Festival. Tears of joy ran down all our cheeks.

CHAPTER EIGHT

Golden October

Glorious October is the last month of our trout fishing calendar, and as autumn gathers pace, illustrated so beautifully by the leaves losing their green to be replaced by a dazzling array of browns, we notice for the first time a nip in the early morning air as we gaily scamper down to the lake. The wood smoke that seems to linger as bonfires glitter in the late afternoons adds to a time of expectancy of something more to come as one enjoys a first delicious shiver as soon as the sun begins to wane shortly after mid-afternoon. The water has never looked clearer, yet our flies, poor imitations of nature's wondrous originals, look very manufactured and lifeless as they are gently drawn back in a lacklustre attempt at animation. Fewer fish are caught, blanks are common, and many a net remains dry.

The advice I offer at this time of the year is to halve the breaking strength of the leader, thereby reducing the diameter of the line to make it less likely to be seen by the quarry, and lower the size of fly offered, again to reduce the chance of the fish becoming suspicious to the point of refusing the offering. Also, the speed of retrieval has to be constantly altered, from criminally quickly to ridiculously slowly, in the hope of inducing a take. And, lastly, if by chance one has to suffer the gloomy and pessimistic rote of pulling a lure, then let it be of the fry variety, as for the last week both browns and rainbows have developed a taste for the fry of the indigenous coarse fish.

Mort and I had arrived at the lake mid-morning in order to take advantage of the most propitious fishing opportunities between ten and three of the clock, as either side of these times seems oddly quiet at this time of year. Although we left the happy home under something of a cloud, I fervently hoped my ogress back at the cottage would have mellowed by the time we arrived home, and I naturally blamed Mort, as the idea had been his.

I had been pacing the hall that morning awaiting the arrival of my dearest friend before departing for a last hurrah of the season at Star Lake, as the water closes today, October the sixteenth. Hearing voices outside, I found Mort deep in conversation with the hellcat herself. She was at the top of an extending ladder repointing one of the ornate chimneys at the gable end of the building, and I was mortified to see that every time the wind caught her skirt, Mort licked his lips in avid appreciation of her sinewy calves and grotesquely muscled thighs. The awful cad then offered to support the ladder whilst she descended, leering lasciviously all the while until she planted her large and powerful feet onto the gravel. She enjoyed every minute of the intimate examination and raked her sharp, claw-like nails down Mort's cheeks, drawing blood, all the while running a serpent's tongue across her bright red lips, something which was sickening and exciting in equal measure.

Mort seemed hypnotised, so I cannoned my steel toecap sharply onto his knee, a sound and proven method of securing someone's attention, and sure enough he collapsed as if poleaxed and writhed rather too much I thought, as I had deliberately not broken the patella. Getting painfully to his feet, he glared at me like a gorgon and smiled winningly at the lady of the house, asking her if there were any further assistance he could offer, whereas I bridled and withdrew my foot, this time to make contact with his vitals for the offence offered to the hag. She had other ideas though, and swung the mortar pointing iron in her hand sharply across my temple, plunging me into darkness.

I regained consciousness with my head nestled in Mort's foul groin as he tenderly stroked my forehead. The fetid stench from his polluted trousers was repulsive and I instinctively gagged and vomited onto his shirt. I then did the only thing possible under the circumstances; I gripped him by crutch and throat and hurled him bodily for the third time that year into the ornamental pond at the front of the cottage, once again apologising to the resident carp for this rank intrusion into their watery world.

Emerging from his dousing in a rather combative manner, Mort advanced, and I again did the only thing I could and whacked him heartily about the head with the aluminium rod tube I had spotted in the porch. Sure enough, the surly beast recognised his master and touched his cap in the correct serf-to-gentleman manner, becoming agreeable once more. He explained that before stamping away, the crone had informed him of the need for the chimneys to be swept. She had noted the accumulation of soot whilst attending to the pointing and had inquired of him if he knew of a reputable sweep. He had then offered to clean the stacks and flues, as he was vastly experienced in their care and maintenance. Having agreed a price she had stalked off, promising to return before lunch to inspect his handiwork.

There followed a moment of silence as I contemplated committing bloody murder to this ignorant, malodorous runt, but I quickly retracted my doubts as he outlined the method he had used successfully in the past. I would ascend the roof, and Mort would be below ready with drapes. A weighted sweep's brush would then be dropped down the chimney and caught, and the resultant fallen soot collected, bagged and sold for profit to the allotment association, where it was to be added to the compost heap, thus enriching it. He estimated each chimney would be done in twenty minutes, and as there were but six, that would leave us plenty of time to repair to the lake. I stared in wondrous admiration at this adorable man, for in half a morning we would have silver in our pocket, the witch in good humour and the rest of the day to enjoy some fishing.

Having gained the roof, I released the weighted brush down the first chimney, receiving the all-clear from Mort below. However a strange foreboding and a sense of panic began to gnaw at the base of my stomach as Mort's echoing, distorted voice came out of the chimney pot to the right of the one I had dropped the brush down, telling me again to release the weight.

A cold sweat broke out on my brow as my suspicion grew about what had just occurred. I scampered down the ladder and flew into the house, where I saw Mort in the fireplace of the spotless sitting room with his head up the chimney and mechanically turned my head toward the closed portal of the dining room. With a shaking hand I grasped the beautiful baroque knob and thrust open the door in one swift movement.

One glance into that murky atmosphere was enough to induce a panic the like of which my heart had never known before. Everything was now the colour of ebony, as if a large charcoal-laden brush brandished by some mad artist had been applied to the whole interior, and a sable mist of inky particles was slowly settling. Mort, appearing noiselessly at my side, took in the stygian scene, patted my arm, grinned toothlessly and said all would be well, and to meet him in the car in ten minutes to depart for Star Lake. With leaden legs I obeyed my unsightly, misshapen would-be saviour, and limped out to wait in the Bentley. When he appeared presently, carrying a small grimy sack, I failed to comment, merely staring woodenly through the windscreen as I contemplated the horrors my wife would unleash upon me when we returned.

Mort drove sedately to the lake with me sitting in

a blue funk, my teeth rattling like castanets in my head. On arrival, he opened a hip flask decorated with the pithy motto *'Vive et vivere permitte'* (live and let live). Then he poured a concoction of his own distilling, still warm from his flabby buttock, down my throat. This libation of liquor turned my stomach into a furnace and caused sweat to pour down my face. I gasped for air, clutching my throat, as Mort explained the ingredients of this most powerful potation. Swede, raisins and sugar were the main constituents, with the addition of his favoured benzene providing the mule-like kick, and his final ministration was to push the cork handle of my favourite fly-rod into my wet palm. The combination of pure alcohol and piscatorial vibrations immediately worked on my fevered soul, so that as we pushed out our final boat for the season there was a smile on my face and I felt a debt of gratitude to the clod pulling lustily at the oars, for though he was imbecilic at times, I loved him for the giant puppy-like blundering bruiser he was.

I caught none that afternoon, but as the light began to fade, Mort struck to a gentle take on a skilfully-fished Olive Palmer. Time and again the fish took line until, exhausted, it slipped into the net, revealing a brown trout of truly dazzling hues, its red and black spots in gorgeous contrast to the regal golden-brown flanks. Not quite two pounds, it was the most splendid sight, and I was glad that Mort refused to kill it, merely holding it carefully upright in the water until, with a flick of the tail, it shot into the blue-green depths.

I was at peace, and as Mort rowed quietly back, I failed to see him noiselessly deposit the grimy sack from the house over the stern and into the wash of our small wake.

On arrival back at the cottage, we were greeted with pandemonium. The fire appliance bathed all in its rotating bright blue light as the villagers, held back by the plump, rotund form of our very own Constable Laurel, pressed forward, shouting enquiries. Uniformed members of the brigade were industriously rolling and stowing water hoses onto the tender as my brutal bride burst out of the front door accompanied by some senior figure from the emergency services. The man was evidently both terrified and alarmed by the beldam I now had my arm around and as I continued to soothe and stroke her, he gave me a verbatim report of the incident. It would appear that the log fire that had been lit against the autumn chill had ignited a large bird's nest in the dining room chimney. I opened my mouth to speak, but desisted as he continued to explain that a portion of half-burnt nest lying in the hearth would substantiate his theory, as would the profusion of soot distributed around the room, deposited as the nest rolled down the chimney, sweeping all before it, as it were. I turned to speak to Mort, but was not surprised to find he had already melted into the dark and ancient woods.

CHAPTER NINE

Codwalloping

I find November an exciting and very full month. Not content with the anniversary of the discovery of the Gunpowder Plot, it also manages to fit in Martinmas, All Hallows, honouring all the saints first observed in AD835, All Souls' Day, the supplication for all the souls in purgatory and Thanksgiving Day, the fourth Thursday, if one is unfortunate enough to have been born under American skies. It also includes Star Lake's annual sea fishing trip.

The trout season having concluded in October, we are bereft of fishing until the pike cull in December and January. Angling withdrawal symptoms including headache, nausea, constipation or diarrhoea, falling heart rate and blood pressure, fatigue, drowsiness and insomnia, irritability, difficulty concentrating and anxiety. Any suffering this dreadful malaise should arm themselves with a boat rod and join this most holy of crusades, which this year was bound for Whitby.

Tonight, All Hallows Eve, the night when more than at any other time of the year the ghosts of the dead are able to mingle with the living, my wife was abroad in the village accompanied by her dark hound Seyton, more likely than not bringing terror and sleepless nights to those unfortunate souls who crossed her path. Mort and I however were cheery and warm in the magnificently-appointed cottage snug. The log fire that blazed in the iron basket crackled and roared as we bathed in the cheery glow reflected from the iron backplate, which carried the motto *'illegitimi non carborundum'* (don't let the bastards grind you down). Shadows danced eerily on ancient pine panelling as the smoke from our briars curled lazily upwards to be lost amongst the venerable beams. Mort spat forcefully into the flames, and we started violently as the ball of phlegm exploded on contact with the blaze. He sat transfixed as a jet of flame, a heady mixture of distilled parsnip wine and benzene, shot towards his groin. With a cry, he began beating his trousers as the conflagration leapt towards his filthy shirt tails, but a masterly turn of mine with the soda siphon soon drenched his apparel and choked the fire, leaving him singed, faintly steaming and not for the first time regretting his choice of drink.

The moment soured and the evening spoiled, Mort repaired for the spinster Arkwright's outhouse, where he temporarily lodged, and I looked again to the details of our fishing trip planned for the middle of the month. Twenty-two were booked, including myself, Mort, my wife, the Moriarty sisters, Farmer Wright *et al*. The coach from Bayleaf the gardener's cousin was arranged and breakfast booked at the Marigold Café, overlooking the harbour. I sat back in the worn but comfortably cracked leather armchair and was immediately lost in the fantasy of a piscatorial adventure off the coast of north Yorkshire.

The cod is one of Britain's most sought-after sea fish, especially during the winter months. Whether filleted and battered, baked into a pie or poached in milk, it is delicious. We should expect weights of up to eight pounds, but five would be more realistic, and in reality codling of one to two pounds on light tackle will give a good account of themselves. Cod much prefer cold water, so they will be closer into our shores than in the summer, and with that happy thought, my very fibre began to tingle with anticipation.

The spell was broken, however, when the door to the snug flew open, propelled by a large hobnail-booted foot, and crashed against the wall. Framed in the light from the hall stood the virago to whom I was wed and by her side, with slavering jaws and red rimmed hellish eyes, her foul hound. I looked into her eyes and saw madness, and knew with sick dread that the moon was full and I must yet again submit to our periodic lovemaking. She threw me over her shoulder and as she trudged on enormous hairy feet in the direction of the bedchamber, I slipped into unconsciousness.

In the morning, having burnt the ripped and soiled bed linen, I lay in some discomfort from the multitude of bruises and small cuts which she had, in her passion, inflicted upon my body. In the antique claw-footed bath, the rising steam scented with lavender and rosemary did little to calm my mind as I yet again pondered being married to this beast. As usual I arrived at no particular conclusion, save that in the event of her insanity becoming permanent, rather than manifesting at twenty-eight day intervals, I would, as an act of kindness, be forced to cull her, like the pike in Star Lake.

Sighing, I rose from the perfumed water and went in search of breakfast and grilled kidneys, finding both in the rotund and chunky presence of Susan, the maid.

She appeared as dumpy and corpulent as usual, but the huskiness in her voice and the colour in her cheeks suggested a recent encounter with Mort. There was a ripe, unpleasant odour, redolent of a warm, sweaty Stilton, and I knew my friend lurked nearby.

Filling a breakfast plate, I put it on the end of the refectory table and grinned as a scruffy, seedy, greatcoated figure edged around the dining room door. Dirty fingerless mittens over grime-laden fingers clutched the platter to his decrepit face as he breathed in the heady aroma of sausages, kidneys and bacon, and no word could not be extracted from him whilst he gurgled and gasped, panted and gulped down the meal. At last, pushing away the plate and emitting a gargantuan belch, he counted himself ready to discuss that evening's bonfire in celebration of the foiling of the Gunpowder Plot and in aid of much-needed funds for the repair of the Reverend Farthing's organ.

Guy, or Guido, Fawkes broke his neck whilst trying to escape execution and therefore evaded the horror of hanging, drawing and quartering. This assuaged my boredom not one wit as the umpteenth rocket fizzed and whooshed to the heavens, which were split asunder with the resultant detonation, and one's ears were then assailed by an explosion not dissimilar to that of a Mills bomb, a grooved cast-iron hand grenade with a central striker held by a closed hand lever and secured with a pin. The Baratol filling was subject to either a four or seven-second fuse, and was quite devastating at close quarters. Others were obviously affected by the fireworks as Constable Laurel led both the Brigadier and Fraser, the fish farmer, away in some agitation. Old war horses both, it took but a whiff of cordite to transport them back to the battlefield.

Squire Elliott, who owned the slaughterhouse on the outskirts of the village, was selling prime ribs and burgers, whilst Davies the greengrocer roasted potatoes in Miss Arkwright's pottery kiln and in an old tin bath he had prepared gallons of mushy peas that were divinely flavoured with black pepper and fresh mint from Bayleaf's garden.

Mort was sole proprietor of the drink stall and was doing a brisk trade in tea, coffee and distilled parsnip wine. I was appalled, as the strength of this fiery spirit made it lethal to the untrained drinker, and many were the people who had imbibed and were now struggling to keep their feet. One of that number was the Reverend Farthing, who had been granted the task of lighting the village bonfire. He wove his way unsteadily towards that very pile, walked past the enormous heap of wood and plunged his burning brand into the thatch of Cowie's cottage instead. The dwelling, which had remained empty since the lowly swineherd had fled the village in terror and craven cowardice, erupted into flame.

Whatever unspoken message communicated itself to the villagers that night, it has never been referred to. In stony, immoveable silence they watched the midden burn to the ground, as if to vouchsafe their collective opinion of the mongrel that once dwelt there, and to this day, an overgrown tangle of vegetation is the only marker of the spot.

As our brightly-coloured charabanc pulled gaily into Whitby, two dozen eager piscators strained for a view of the sea. The weather however was dour, with dark clouds scudding over a battleship-grey sky. We repaired to the Marigold Café for a traditional fry-up before setting sail, and requested that everything be fried in dripping, as the lady in charge had told Mort that a lining of grease on the gut is imperative when sailing. I limited my intake to dry toast and a cup of red Ginseng tea, as I have endured motion sickness, or sea sickness, but once. On that occasion I came as close to dying as if I were already in the rowing boat and crossing the river Styx, that boundary between the living and the dead. I have never felt so wretched in my entire life.

The proprietress of the café, a pudgy, thickset woman with blackheads round her eyes, pressed upon us slices of pork pie to stave off hunger and bade us farewell and good luck. As we motored toward the entrance of the harbour, she continued waving until she was lost to view. The mood aboard the *Whitby Lass* was one of gaiety, that is until the skipper cleared the haven and put us into the wind. The sea, which had been quite tranquil in the dock, now seemed wild and rough. Huge troughs opened before us into which we repeatedly disappeared, to feebly crawl to the next crest, only to tumble quickly into the following trough as we fought towards the fishing grounds eight to twelve miles out. Most of the party's complexions ranged from ashen white to pale green around the gills as they fought to keep down the contents of their stomachs, and even I paled as the skipper said the motion would become more disturbing when he cut the engines so that we could fish for the cod.

He kindly reduced the charter from six to three hours, and only five of us stood upright on the deck as the *Whitby Lass* scurried towards her anchorage. A dozen and a half men and women lay in the gunwales feebly choking and coughing, exhorting those who were still able to end their misery with a quick and merciful death. Mort, with barely the strength to stand, staggered up the harbour steps, grasped the crone from the café between throat and gusset and hurled her into the harbour.

Those of us who were able to angle carried off five stones of cod, which was good fishing. We had merely seen another face of the ocean. Competent trout anglers we may be, but that day we tipped our caps most respectfully to our brothers who harvest the saltwater and the skippers who escort them.

CHAPTER TEN

The Holly and the Ivy

December is the first month of the meteorological winter in the Northern Hemisphere and the twenty-first of the month has the shortest daylight hours of the year. The lights of the Victorian cottage in which we dwell seemed to be on all day, such was the gloom from the leaden skies. Whilst not in the least snowy, the still air was cold and frigid, with plunging temperatures overnight and sharp frosts, hardening both ground and water alike.

We had recovered from the painful sea fishing trip to Whitby, which strangely had not dampened our enthusiasm but whetted our collective appetites for the briny medium. Although by next year, we resolved to be prepared more thoroughly. I have requested several definitive journals on that art from my wife for Christmas, while she has requested a similar number of almanacs and publications on arcane arts, poisonous plants and concealable weaponry of the twentieth century. Physicians and psychiatric practitioners were still not in accord as to whether a sojourn in the asylum near to Fraser's fish farm would prove beneficial for her. I attempted to sway their decisions with subtle bribes, but found the psychiatrists trustworthy and unfortunately, morally upright.

However, all was not doom and gloom, for below the surface of any body of fresh water, amongst the shadowy lanes of weeds and water plants, lies a usually-dormant olive-green fish, shaded from yellow to white along the belly and with a flank that is marked with short light bar-like spots. It is of course the hunter-killer *Esox lucius*, or Northern Pike. There are historic reports of giant pike caught in nets in Ireland in the late 19th century tipping the scales at ninety pounds, but with no photographic evidence or the like, we must be content with the forty-six pound record of our fair isles.

Shaped like a torpedo with most of its fins set back towards the tail, this assassin is built for explosive speed. It has sensory pores on its head and lower jaw which are part of the lateral line system and sensitive to vibration, coupled with a large mouth liberally filled with rear-pointing teeth. The pike is the perfect executioner of fish. This cold-hearted butcher can be vital for keeping a balance, as weak, deceased or injured fish are not welcome in the water, and so the pike is feted, admired and angled for, as we at Star Lake strive to keep that balance right ere he takes too many hale and hearty trout in the summer months.

After a hard period of frost an appearance by the sun raises the water temperature two or three degrees, pressing a switch in the pike's slightly flattened, elongated skull, and suddenly he feels hunger. With a gentle flick of his powerful tail, he propels himself through the murky depths towards his prey. He now becomes hunted as well as hunter, for this is when Piscator is at his most deadly and the pike at his most vulnerable.

Animated conversation rang around the lake as we gathered in front of the lodge to receive final instructions from the Wing Commander on the day's pike fishing, the first of four to be held during the month of December. All pike caught were to be placed alive in the nearest tank relative to one's position, six tanks having been positioned along the banks. These fish were to be donated to Squire Elliott, the slaughterhouse owner, who also had an interest in a catfish lake in the adjoining parish. I involuntarily shook my head at this, and Mort sucked his yellowed teeth in sympathy as we pictured the noble trout in comparison to the hideous, bottom-dwelling, carrion-eating denizen of the squires' water. The pike were to be additional sport for the many anglers plying their art at his lake, and I shuddered as I remembered Mort telling me of nightly migrations by these fearsome catfish, which are able to propel themselves over land by judicious use of their fins.

I chided myself for a fool for entertaining such fears and planted a well-timed kick to Mort's fetid backside for putting them there in the first place. He picked himself up and rushed me, but I adroitly side-stepped and again booted his behind, this time the steel in my hob nails eliciting a cry of pain, and before he could rise, I had positioned the hook of my telescopic gaff above his carotid artery. With a nod, he accepted my superiority, and I gallantly hauled him to his feet, whereby he called me a gentleman, and all enmity fled as we began to fish the lake in earnest, dearest friends once more.

I opted for a gaily painted Mepps spinning lure, whilst Mort resorted to his favoured method of freelined deadbait. For the next two hours we hiked the banks, casting hither and yon, until a dull report from the Brigadier's little cannon echoed across the lake, signalling lunch. For the gift of any pike caught, Squire Elliott gave thanks by providing spare rib chops and freshly-made sage sausages for a fine barbecue, expertly cooked by the Moriarty sisters.

Although during the morning Mort and I remained fishless, others fared better. Seven pike were taken, with the largest at eleven pounds falling to Constable Laurel's artfully-presented little dead roach. Thus, with an eye on the sun, which had already begun its descent down an azure sky, I decided to ape the pot-bellied, thickset policeman's tactic, and fish a deadbait under a bung float. Mort, though ignorant and uneducated, is yet possessed of an innate atavistic skill in the pursuit of a quarry, and under his expert guidance, I carefully mounted a whole herring on a rig comprising three mercilessly-sharp treble hooks, and again under his direction, we stealthily made our way towards the deepest part of the lake in the corner of the railway bank.

The herring struck the water with a dull plop and sank out of sight below the brightly-painted float, and Mort and I settled down to wait, both of us casting anxious glances at a sky which was rapidly darkening as the early nightfall drew nearer.

The float disappeared in an instant, and I gaped open-mouthed at the space on the water which had been occupied by it. With a curse, Mort wrapped a filthy hand around the rod where the cork handle ended and quickly raised the point, savagely setting home the hooks. The fish took off towards the centre of the lake, and I cried in pain as the handle struck my hand. Mort gave a cry of triumph and shouted down my ear that the pike, for that was what we assumed it must be, had made a mistake by not running for the bank and a submerged log to which many a piscator had lost flies.

There followed ten long minutes of heart-stopping runs by the fish, and frantic retrieves as I sought to master this titan. My knees sagged when I first caught sight of the behemoth that surfaced and struggled as Mort reached out with the gaff at the water's edge.

At over forty inches long, I reckoned the pike could possibly be a record fish, and if not, then it should still be cased and mounted in my fishing shed. I mentally lost count of the good folk from the club who would pass my portal, wishing to admire the capture and patting my shoulder with delight and envy in equal proportions. But then Mort awoke me from my woolgathering with an imprecation to keep the line tight as he had yet to set the gaff. In an instant, the giant weight on the rod and line was gone. The pike rolled on the surface, fixed me with a baleful glare, and vanished.

Mort attacked me as if possessed, shouting and screaming my stupidity, and members rushed to save us from each other, as I in turn was attempting foul and bloody damage upon the moron who had failed to gaff my greatest fish, until we were parted and sedated. Luckily old Doctor Bell was fishing that day, and thus we were dispatched quickly to the asylum next to the hatchery and fish farm for observation and evaluation.

We were released in time for Christmas and sat down together to a festive lunch of Norfolk Black turkey and all the trimmings. Susan, our chubby, heavy-set maid and cook, had surpassed herself by creating a divinely savoury stuffing of sage, rosemary, Marmite and distilled spirit, perfectly complementing the pigs in blankets, and by the time we retired to the comfortable lounge, that Homeric harmony between Mort and me that a mere fish could never erase for long had been restored. Presents were given and received and Seyton, my wife's devilish hound, never growled once at me, for which I was grateful.

The Gorgon herself presented me with a treatise on pike fishing, and I could see no trace of sarcasm on her drably-painted face, merely the usual distaste for my company intermingled with a frisson of boredom. From my dearest friend, a battered small silver box, in which to keep a few flies and inscribed '*amittere non potest quod nec antea*' (you cannot lose what you never had), and of course he was right, I had no claim on the leviathan that still silently roamed his watery kingdom, but I vowed we would meet again in the New Year and that this time, I would be the one to triumph. Mort raised his glass of powerful, golden parsnip spirit and I knew that he too harboured that same desire to net the monster. Angling does that to a chap.

CHAPTER ELEVEN

In with the New

I lay as still as was possible in the confines of the narrow camping bed in my shed, clutching my head tightly with both hands in an effort to contain the constant throbbing pain in my temples caused by the foul stench that emanated from the prostrate carcase that lay huddled in the wheelbarrow at the foot of my cot. A working hypothesis suggested I must be hung over and Mort was his usual self. I struggled to recall what had occurred the previous evening at the New Year's Eve party at the vicarage, hosted by the Reverend Farthing. He is a trusting soul and had quickly agreed to Mort supplying the libations for the evening. What he was unaware of was Mort's recent success in increasing the alcohol level in the output of his distilling apparatus to a shade over one hundred and fifty proof. This strength would incapacitate an elephant and thus easily felled the partygoers.

Staggering over to the fly-tying bench, I began ministrations with pestle and mortar and had soon powdered sufficient willow bark to treat both Mort and myself. I then tottered up the garden path with a wobbling wheelbarrow before depositing him once more in the now familiar ornamental fountain. The thin ice broke easily as his rancid, contaminated hulk splashed into the water. With a monstrous roar, he erupted from the water, fixed me with a warlike glare and advanced. My cranial pain was too much too bear, so I disabled him quickly and without mercy with a vicious jab to the solar plexus, then swung him, groaning, over my shoulder and repaired to the shed, where the pain-relieving and anti-inflammatory effects of the salicin within the willow bark, mixed with a little parsnip wine, soothed the horrors of our combined hangovers, thereby allowing the clarity of thought we needed to prepare for another foray to Star Lake in pursuit of the huge pike we had managed to lose in early December.

The constant study of an almanac of pike-fishing my wife had bought me for Christmas had given me a decent grounding in that arm of our majestic pastime. I combined that with absorbing facts and ideas from various chronicles and journals, reinforcing the notion that another encounter with the monster pike was surely guaranteed. The atmospheric circumstances were identical, with the temperature rising three degrees in the morning after a prolonged cold and icy snap, and it was in a highly-excited state that we consumed that morning's kidneys prepared by the stout maid Susan. Only once did Mort's begrimed and blackened paw creep furtively under that portly girl's short tartan skirt.

Shortly afterwards, we were barrelling down white and frozen lanes in the supercharged Bentley, the frigid air howling and streaming our eyes to tears as the open-topped tourer bounced and rattled over innumerable ruts and potholes in the surface of the byway. I vowed on our return to once again importune the local council to cease patching and mending the tarmacadam and renew the entire surface. Turning to Mort and expecting his assent, I was startled to see his eyelids had frozen shut and that an icicle of mucus was adorning his snout. Stopping quickly, I remembered an old Berber trick, and pulling his hip flask from his revolting, unwashed trousers, I liberally sprinkled his face with methylated spirits. Igniting the same, I sat back to observe the results. I thought the theory was that only the fumes would burn, thereby safely thawing his face out. However, when his eyebrows and hair also caught fire, I was forced to grab him by the throat and groin and hurl him, wailing, into a snowdrift at the side of the road. I rapidly leapt out of the car to assist the now-weeping Mort, although I noted with interest that both his eyelids and proboscis were now defrosted. I remain convinced of the efficacy of igniting those close to us if and when the need should arise.

All that late morning and afternoon, Mort quietly rowed us up and down the deep water before the railway bank, and for extra stealth, that wily old piscator had muffled the oars in the rowlocks by clever use of a dozen scarves purloined from the vast collection of accessories my wife keeps to disguise her wattle-like throat. Once I gobbled like a turkey as she arranged her neckwear and received such a boxing of the ears that they rang for days.

As the sun set and a rapidly-cooling twilight descended upon the lake, we reflected on the day with the other rods who had fished. The Wing Commander, Miss Arkwright and the brigadier had all caught small pike to eight pounds, whereas Farmer Wright, the

Squire and Doctor Bell had blanked. Mort and I had enjoyed some sport with a pike apiece, but nothing remotely as heavy as our pre-Christmas encounter. As Bayleaf lit the storm lanterns, the Moriarty sisters served a light meal of Irish stew and cabbage and Mort circulated with a sweet parsnip tipple designed to warm rather than intoxicate. As a warm feeling of camaraderie spread amongst this most happy of bands, I again gave thanks to the piscatorial deity from whom all fishing adventures flow.

The next morning as the harpy and I finished breakfast, I leant across to fill her cup from the cafetière and froze as a warning growl issued from the throat of Seyton, that vile and intimidating cur that accompanies her wherever she goes. I was relieved to realise that the object of his enmity was Todd, the dim-witted postman, who was plodding up the gravelled drive with a vacant expression on his simple, pockmarked face. I met him at the door in response to the Westminster chime which rang as he pressed the bell-push, and intently examined his face for any sign that he knew what was in the small package he held. I believed that on occasion, when the fey fancy was upon him, he would steam open certain mail items. I could prove nothing, but over the years, the odd damp flap or corrugation along the adhesive border had revealed his guilt. If I thought he had had foreknowledge of this delivery, I would have no alternative but to cull him and bury him in the woods. His brow however, remained clear, and with trembling hand I signed for the small packet and repaired immediately to the shed.

I sat in my favourite armchair and regarded the package with an unblinking eye, wondering again if I was about to cross the Rubicon for what was contained in that innocent brown wrapping paper, for my immortal soul could well be at issue. The instructions for use were written in neat copperplate on the reverse as was the warning in Latin 'cave quid volunt' (be careful what you wish for).

My need for a charm or fetish had begun the day the mighty pike had freed itself from my hooks, and finally, from my bloodshot eyes, and changes in appetite and sleep patterns, I appreciated that I had become some sort of addict. The deterioration of my personal grooming habits and unusual smells on my breath, body and clothing, coupled with tremors and slurred speech, all indicated a craving for that indescribable feeling of euphoria as I battled the fish for supremacy. I needed to catch that pike, and to that end I had finally succumbed to enlisting outside assistance in the form of my wife's Uncle Samuel, a diviner, warlock and occultist, a man of power and intelligence, a maker of spells and an answer to my problem, or a direct route to piscatorial damnation for crossing the boundary between what is morally acceptable and what is not.

For a whole hour did I stare at the innocent little parcel, until a timid tapping awoke me from my reverie and I opened the door to behold the bucolic, rustic features of Susan, who bade me take an urgent telephone call from the lake. I bounded up the path to the cottage and grabbed the receiver to my ear to hear the raucous, harsh tones of Mort spewing from the instrument. He begged me to attend him at the lake with all speed, and no, he would not elaborate as to the nature of the emergency.

In less than five minutes, the Bentley was pointed towards the lake, the supercharger screaming as she hurtled down the lanes in an attempt to reach her destination in record time. I succeeded, slewing into the car park at the side of the lodge just fourteen minutes after leaving the house. Unfortunately, one of the many ducks that reside at the lake and regularly gather at the lodge for titbits cannoned off the front bumper and was dead before it hit the ground. Too agitated to remove the deceased drake, I hurried to where Mort signalled frantically from the field bank of the lake, and found him on his knees staring fixedly at the water, or more accurately, at the cadaver of a very large pike which was gently nudging the bank with every wavelet. She had been dead for some time, the missing eye and large pecked and gnawed holes in her flank mute testament to the work of hungry scavengers, and when Mort threw the corpse over the stranded wire fence into the field, it almost split in two. As we repaired to the car, I revealed all to Mort between the gasps and sobbing, exposing myself for the vain charlatan I truly was. Slow simpleton that he is, laid his simian arm around my shoulders and explained my innocence, in that the charm still sat in my fishing shed and all would be well. Before he climbed into the driving seat, he picked up the body of the duck and stuck it down the front of his trousers.

A phone call from Mort to a certain alchemist ensured silence from that quarter, for no matter how powerful a man of arcane arts may be, to invite a midnight visit from that particular nightmare would be foolhardy indeed. As I relaxed in the cracked and split leather armchair, Mort fried the succulent duck breasts for our supper. He slipped a certain small parcel into the flames of the log-burner as he was doing so. Not that I escaped with dignity intact, as the next day Mort laid all before the Reverend Farthing, who, after admonishment and extracting a promise of atonement from me, presented me with a black eye from an astonishing right hook that whipped me off my feet. As I shook my head and grinned at the priest, I knew it was it was so very good to be amongst friends.

CHAPTER TWELVE

A Poacher, and a Duel

February is from the Latin *febris*, or fever, due to the similar nature of purification or purging from sweating, commonly seen in association with agues and the like, contracted more frequently than at any other time of the year. I was indeed perspiring with fear, for to be abroad in the woods around Star Lake at midnight was a most daunting affair, even for one as daring and heroic as I.

The Wing Commander had called an extraordinary meeting of the membership of the trout fishing syndicate to discuss the most serious matter of poaching. Up until the nineteenth century, as long as a little wildlife and not game was illegally taken by hungry peasants, something of a blind eye was turned. However, when an eagle-eyed member of our happy syndicate espied a Pennell worm tackle hanging from a branch overhanging the lake, then it was deemed theft, pure and simple. This fact was affirmed by our stout and portly law enforcement officer, Police Constable Laurel, a member of our elite little band. Having congratulated ourselves upon the fortune of having a village bobby in our ranks, we were shocked when he called for volunteers to patrol the banks for the rascals, and when no such help had stepped forward, he invoked Rule Seventeen, calling upon all able-bodied members to unite and lend aid against a common foe.

I am counted more valorous and fearless than most, but the mere thought of surprising a thug with a cosh in the dark woods unnerved me to the extent that my stomach churned noisily and I glanced round sharply lest anyone had heard it. Mort shot his hand and mine rapidly into the air whilst chopping the granite-hard edge of his hand savagely into my kidneys, thereby staunching any protest I might raise. He later confessed that by volunteering first, we would ensure the prime choice of watches, and immediately chose the twelve-through-two option, as his experience in the Sherwood Forresters regiment had taught. Thus we found ourselves surreptitiously and furtively stealing through the black, menacing woods. I expected silence and was stunned at how noisy the night was, from the sighing of the wind through willows and rushes to the many and varied sounds as all the nocturnal animals go about their business.

Thankfully, the ladies' arm of our club was barred from attendance, as an encounter with a blackguard was unthinkable for one of the weaker sex, although I thought an encounter with my fearsome wife would make me sympathetic towards the thief. However, all this was forgotten as we noiselessly patrolled the perimeter of the lake, with Mort circling in a clockwise direction and myself in the opposite rotation.

Suddenly, out of the darkness, came the harsh cry of a vixen calling to her mate, the agreed signal that Mort had come across a poacher. I responded with the flat bark of the dog Reynard and was instantly hobbling along the bank. In daylight it appeared as flat as a billiard table, but at night it was as rough as a Bulldog's chin.

Abruptly a load moan carried on the air and I realised with dread that Mort might have been injured, as the scoundrel would hardly call attention to his position. Another, closer, injurious sound made me pause as I stared hard into the blackness and called Mort's name, simultaneously hearing retreating footsteps running down the bank. He groaned and I knew I had located him, as I was forcibly struck by the foul, foetid stench of unwashed body odour. I retched and heaved, violently emptying my stomach, and turned on my million-candlepower torch to see Mort wiping my vomit from his face, revealing a ghastly welt over his eye, from which gore was freely flowing. Apologising for my slight *faux pas*, I allowed him to clutch feebly onto my arm whilst I purposefully led him to the lodge.

Somewhere between the site of the assault and the lodge I shook off his arm in order to scratch my nose, and a tremendous splash followed as Mort took a header into the lake. With the aid of my Ogden's powerful portable searchlight, I soon located him and with clear and lucid instructions directed him to shore. As the immersion had neutralised his natural scent and washed away the puke, I considered it seemly to support him more fully, and with resort to the first aid kit and a quantity of fierce alcohol from the hipflask back at the lodge, I drew a close to our adventures for the night.

The next morning dawned bright and fresh, and Constable Laurel, on his haunches by the lakeside, pulled absently at a fleshy, sensuous lip whilst staring vacantly across the water, the sunlight adding an incongruous gaiety to a scene of violence. Absently scratching his enormous and corpulent rear end, he gave his verdict. The villain had been a man of average height and weight and had probably been wearing either new or freshly-repaired shoes, as neither toe nor heel marks in the mud had shown signs of wear. The identity of the culprit was presumably Josiah Hardwick, as a medallion with a broken chain lay in the churned mud and on one side was his name, while on the other was his family motto, *Ego quod volo* (I do what I want), a most endearing sentiment, but one that failed to touch my heart, which had temporarily turned to stone in light of the savage attack on my greatest companion.

Laurel was all for arresting the bounder immediately, but I needed to confront the sewer rat and discover why he had so roughly transgressed all the unwritten laws on what becomes a gentleman and piscator. Not wishing to get too close to Mort, as he had dried after his dip in the lake and was becoming somewhat pungent once more, I raised my hand in farewell and pointed the Bentley towards Sedgebrook Lake, where Hardwick's motley fly fishing cronies generally disported themselves, and found him spinning a small Devon minnow from a cheap rod in search of pike.

Even the predators of Sedgebrook are thin and undernourished, as if to testify to the poor quality of the water. The five young jacks laid out on the bank would struggle to make a weight of ten pounds between them, but Hardwick assured me that they would be tasty and nourishing in a pie. Unable to make a suitable comment, I watched in silence as he showed some skill with the rude tackle and nodded in appreciation as the rod bent to a hard take from a fish. The struggle that followed was unusually vigorous for a pike, a fish which is normally winded after the first dashes, and my suspicions were confirmed as Josiah bent to net a nice trout of about three pounds. I was as stunned, for the trout to which he had so swiftly applied his priest, being out of season, should have been returned unharmed to the water. I demanded an explanation for his damnable behaviour both here and last night, and was rewarded with the curling of a cruel, thin lip and a shrug of the shoulders. I could tolerate such vile behaviour no longer, and demanded satisfaction, after slapping him hard across both florid cheeks.

The last recorded duel fought in England where one of the participants died took place in eighteen fifty-two, and although I was in no mood to add to that record, a rush of blood had forced me to issue the challenge, and I was astonished when he accepted. He said that as I had a beautiful home, first-class fishing and a fabulously attractive wife, I had the most to lose and would probably withdraw the challenge. Hotly disagreeing with the spouse remark, I remembered my future father-in-law promising two acres and a cow as dowry; I still await the two acres.

Back at the cottage I reported all to Mort, who chortled hard and long and produced his hip flask with a flourish, in order to toast the occasion with a libation of his finest potato spirit. He promised that all would be well and that he would act as second and master of ceremonies to us both. He returned later that evening with a trout from the freezer, which he baked with a knob of butter and served with flaked almonds, and a light horseradish sauce for piquancy. If it were not for the smell, the foul language, his dishevelled appearance and his lewdness, he would make a fine manservant. I sighed, and went to polish my set of antique flintlocks.

The day of the duel was overcast and cold, which was to be expected in February. A trestle table stood in front of the fishing lodge, covered with a fine white Egyptian linen tablecloth, which, Mort informed us, would be used to wrap the body of the losing protagonist. I thought he was enjoying the whole affair rather too much as he intoned the rules to us both, and he actually grinned as he accepted the lead balls we had chosen from a shallow dish resting next to the ornately-carved box containing the pistols. Pouring a measure of black powder from a flask into both barrels, he dropped the balls into the weapons and lightly tamped a small piece of wadding to contain the deadly combination, all the while pleading that a compromise could be reached if we would but apologise to one another. We opened our mouths to speak, but Mort quickly overrode any forthcoming statements by commanding us to our positions with the admonishment that firing to kill was expected, again with a twinkle in his eye that I found baffling, or then again perhaps he truly is a buffoon.

After pacing the required yardage, I turned and sighted down the barrel, and on seeing the puff of smoke issue from Hardwick's pistol, I lost control of my bowels, pulled the trigger and fainted.

Two pairs of trousers flapped from the makeshift washing line strung between the fishing lodge and flagpole at Star Lake as Hardwick and I stared out across the windswept water. Neither of us had been injured, and whilst Mort bemoaned our poor marksmanship, he said he was proud of our courage, and that none would know the state of our underwear after the affair of honour had been concluded.

Whilst supping the soup Mort had prepared, I thought that whilst we would never be friends, Josiah and I had reached a silent conclusion to our enmity. Yet I would never know why he had been at Star Lake or why he had attacked Mort after such a fashion.

Then, with a start, I felt something hard between my lips as the last of the soup was sipped. I fished in my mouth for the offending object and stared at a lead ball in the palm of my hand. I noted that Hardwick was similarly staring into the depths of his own mug. I quickly looked round for Mort, but he had vanished like a ghost at sunrise.

CHAPTER THIRTEEN

The Ides of March

The day the Romans marked as the middle of the month has sinister connotations, especially when applied to March, but not so at Star Lake, for there it means that there remains barely than a fortnight before we can once more sally forth in search of the loveliest of all fish, the trout. Even the vile hag I share the bed with seems almost feminine in the bright spring light, and her devilish daemonhound almost domesticated, such is the lightness in my heart as the month marches majestically onwards towards opening day at the beginning of April.

I have lost count of the number of occasions when Mort and I have had every possible scrap of gear out of the green oak garden room-cum-shed, with every whipping checked and varnished, every cog and spigot greased on every reel and every fly line teased gently through fingertips looking for imperfections or wear, perhaps provoking a trip to Vasilles, the tackle shop in town, where one can spend an entire afternoon surrounded and cocooned by piscatorial ephemera to all sides. Down the alley next to the old press building, the window is the first thing one sees, with rods and reels, flies and nets all seemingly cluttered and tangled, but with the true window-dresser's skill, they draw one onto the premises to touch, to fondle and to bring a little order to the chaos. By handling such delights anointed with the names of Allcock, Hardy, Farlow et al, we cement ownership, and hang the wallet being a few pounds lighter on the way home. Mort, on the other hand, begins to exhibit conflicting signs, including mood swings, temper and irritability, as the atavistic need to fish weighs heavily upon him. He does not possess my even temperament and general superior emotional control and on occasion will need correction and more rarely, restraint.

I had arrived home unexpectedly and discovered Susan, my wife's simple maid, asleep on the ancient and well-worn chaise longue in the kitchen. I will not tolerate idleness and sharply tipped her onto the slab floor, simultaneously pouring freezing water from a handy carafe onto her plump and homely face and demanding an explanation for her inactivity. She recounted how Mort had worn her out during the morning with his ceaseless demands, and one could quite imagine the context of some of them. One cut across her ample backside with my riding crop had her scurrying from the kitchen in search of my wife, no doubt to complain of my brutal treatment. I take no pleasure punishing those of the lower classes, but one must maintain standards. With a sigh, I went in search of Mort, finding him at last in the small cold store off the kitchen pantry.

What I saw shocked me. Mort crouched in the corner, filthy and naked and chewing listlessly on a salted mackerel in each hand. He stared sightlessly into space whilst saliva ran in rivulets over his putrid carcass. This was possibly the worst case of Angling Withdrawal Syndrome I had ever witnessed. Whilst non-life threatening, it is a terrible malady, besetting the sufferer with debilitating feeblemindedness and eventual total mental collapse. I had read studies, mainly from the German Low Countries, where they are more sympathetic in that they recognise it as a notifiable disease, and quickly took steps to limit the damage the affliction could effect upon poor Mort. I placed a copy of the *Compleat Angler*, that most holy of all angling tomes, into his right hand, and the beautifully-shaped cork handle of his favourite Hardy Bros nine-foot nymph rod into the left. Then I rang the doctor.

Dr Bell's face fell when he entered the cold store and took in Mort's condition. I had laid him on the butcher's block in the middle of the room and covered him with a piece of rough sacking, as our Egyptian cotton sheets are almost impossible to launder if badly soiled, and a nod from the physician as he began to unpack his accoutrements confirmed that he understood my reasoning. If Mort had gone mad, he would probably have had me cull him, rather than let him spend his days as a gibbering wreck. As the good doctor began a fuller examination, I idly wondered as to the best method of despatch, and what to do with the body thereafter.

After some minutes of careful examination, the medico stated himself satisfied that Mort had undergone a total mental collapse and that committal to the asylum up by Fraser's fish farm was the answer. As his signature as healer and mine as a most upstanding member of the local gentry were all that were necessary, Mort was transferred to that grim and forbidding establishment post-haste.

I visited Mort a couple of days later at our very own

Bedlam and was rewarded with a glare reminiscent of a basilisk as he looked up from a sampler he was completing. The stitching was very crude, but the verse touched my heart as it had first done some thirty years previously,

THE ANGLER'S PRAYER *(ORATIOR PISCATOR)*

Lord grant that I may catch a fish
So big that even I
When speaking of it afterwards
Shall have no need to lie

Lord grant that I may live to fish
Until my dying day
And when it comes to my last cast
Then I most humbly pray

When in the good Lord's landing net
And peacefully asleep
That in his mercy I am judged
As good enough to keep.

With trembling hands, I accepted the gift from Mort. I would see it framed and on the privy wall as an inspiration every time I sat there and pondered. With grabbing, claw-like fingers Mort grasped my sleeve and begged me to assist in his escape from this place of confinement, saying that one session of shock treatment had cleared his mind of temporary prostration and he was in neither need nor hurry for a repeat dose of over a hundred volts to the gonads.

Back at the roomy and spacious cottage, I sat deep in thought and pondered how best to assist Mort in his escape and recovery. I smiled as realisation dawned. I would seek direction from a person of very few moral scruples and with a penchant for the seedier side of life, someone who was undaunted by the threat of violence. In short, I went in search of my wife, and was drawn immediately by the caterwauling and shrieking issuing from the well-appointed day-room. On entry, I did not find bloody murder, but instead the hag herself practising on the sackbut, a type of trombone from the Renaissance and Baroque eras designed for choral and vocal music. The sound instilled within me a desire to mutilate the musician who was attempting, and failing, to coax a tune from the instrument. For once I felt pity for the cur Seyton, who lay in abject exhaustion, howling piteously. I could stand neither cacophony any longer, so I wrenched the instrument from my wife and threw it out of the window, closely followed by the snarling hound, who in his rage flew back at the casement seeking my throat. However, a judiciously-lowered sash frame left the devilish mongrel stunned and lying beneath the sill as I turned to the witch.

A medium lead-weighted priest had slipped from the sleeve of her boiler suit into her calloused hand as she demanded the meaning of my intrusion, but she became less warlike as I outlined Mort's condition and predicament. Not for the first time, I noticed vulnerability in her whenever Mort came into the equation, but was astonished when she tossed the greasy curls on her over-large head and laughed long and loudly.

My wife was the foremost member of the East Midlands Sackbut Ensemble and was to play, with her discordant cronies, at the psychiatric facility that housed Mort that very week. She would get me in, the meanwhile keeping all interested parties busy, whilst I heroically rescued my dearest friend and fellow piscator. I was at a loss as to why the authorities would allow people in their care to be subjected to such aural abuse and said as much to the vixen by my side. She boxed my ears violently and ejected me from the house, and I had to flee for the sanctuary of the garden room as Seyton, now recovered, sought his most bloody revenge.

The night of the escape attempt arrived with neither pomp nor ceremony. I delivered the shrew, her chums and the instruments to the institution, helped them set up and then melted into the shadows of the corridors in search of Mort. I found him asleep, and he never awoke as I injected him with a hefty dose of morphine in order to keep any noise down to a minimum, though the harsh and discordant tones from the musicians washing through the building would have covered a mortar going off, and implemented my plan.

I would take him to the place that was most dear to his heart and let Mother Nature soothe his tortured mind with her kindly hand. Thus, after dousing him with a solution of carbolic and quicklime to kill the smell that was emanating in waves from his sweaty body, I rapidly dressed him in his favourite camouflaged overalls and transported him in a wheelbarrow to the Bentley, where I dumped him into the boot and set off to Star Lake in a trice.

As dawn broke and I awoke, the water had never looked so beautiful, with sunlight dappling the small wavelets that gently lapped the shore, evidence of a soft southerly breeze. I sighed in contentment as I absorbed the vista surrounding me, until I was startled out of my reverie by a muffled banging from the boot. As I released the catch, Mort shot out like a cork from a bottle and advanced in a most warlike fashion, arms outstretched like a wrestler as he grabbed me in a painful bear hug and began to squeeze the life out of me. I knew this could not be the rational actions of my dear, true friend, but that he must be still be suffering from the lack of relief and fulfilment only angling can confer, and so I did the only thing I could. Using a manoeuvre taught to me by my wife, I grasped his ears tightly and delivered a ferocious head-butt. There was a nasty crunch as bone and cartilage parted, and Mort went down as if poleaxed. I gingerly dragged him by his hair onto the veranda of the lodge and lightly tied him to one of the Brigadier's old campaign chairs facing the lake before going inside to put the kettle on. All that day I kept him restrained, but only observed peace and tranquillity in him as that bucolic scene and the magic that is spring both worked their wiles upon his dull and simple mind.

As the sun began its descent and the short spring twilight approached, the wind ceased to sigh through the reeds and willows and a hatch of olives produced a rise. The fish were taking the flies off the surface of the water, and the newly-stocked trout went berserk, filling the air with the joyous sounds of fish excitedly gorging themselves.

I loosed Mort's bonds and pressed an old tin mug of his favourite parsnip spirit and a dash of benzene into his gnarled hands. His rheumy red eyes were shining wetly as he nodded his approval at the good work that had been done by the pre-season work parties, attendance at which was a condition of joining our happy piscatorial society. Everything was neat and trimmed and ready for opening day, and as Mort's sinewy arm slid comfortingly around my shoulders, I felt a glow of affection for the old reprobate, and knew further treatment at the asylum would not be needed.

Et fratres in armis, cordium (brothers in arms and hearts)

CHAPTER FOURTEEN

A Cross to Bear

April was halfway through, with winter just a frigid memory as the days perceptibly lengthened, allowing daytime temperatures down at Star Lake to peak at an agreeable sixteen degrees Celsius. Our little trout fishing syndicate was enjoying its best-ever start to the season, with no one having failed to catch during the first fortnight. Even the Wing Commander managed to take a fish, a feat in itself as his previous season's total had been a mere fourteen trout, accumulated over some fifty visits.

Easter Sunday, a week earlier, had fallen on the

sixth of April, and as I lounged in one of the deckchairs in front of the fishing lodge, I remembered promising the Reverend Farthing that Mort and I would dispose of the wooden cross that had formed the mainstay of the Easter procession that had trooped through the village, symbolising Christ's resurrection to eternal life. The cross had been in use for fifty years throughout the parish and was a little dog-eared and worn at the edges, so Davies, the grocer and part-time Sexton, was to procure a new one, and Mort and I would turn the old one into saleable logs for hearths, fireplaces and wood burners the length and breadth of the parish. I chuckled and rubbed my hands together as I pictured the extra income my foul wife would miss, because although we shared our money, my ten percent would never have the purchasing power of her ninety, and a little extra would take care of my pipe tobacco bill very nicely. It brought to mind a long-ago motto, though for the very life of me I could not recall from whence: *radix omnium malorum est cupiditas* (money is the root of all evil).

One of the Moriarty sisters, who were organising teas, mistook my smiling visage for a sign of encouragement, and plastering a smile across her ghastly dial she made to come across the veranda. I was having none of it, and quickly pulled my catapult from the top of my wellington boot. Slipping a quarter-inch ball bearing into the pouch, I let fly with a ripper, right into the fleshy part of her thigh just below her miniskirt. She let out a shriek, clasped her injured limb and fled for the kitchen. My smile broadened further as the Wing Commander at the other end of the balcony nodded his approbation of a fine shot.

After a few moments, the second sister appeared with my Boh tea, the finest Malaysian black, and after a hurried apology with respect to her sibling's behaviour she turned to go, without waiting to hear my acceptance. I again would have none of it and planted my boot forcefully to her scrawny behind, sending her spinning over the railing. The Wing Commander once again nodded his approval to this most necessary action. I strolled over to the balustrade to see if the girl was damaged in any way by her short fall, for though I am a man of the highest moral principles, I am neither cad nor bully.

Peering over the banister, I noted the recumbent form of the angular younger Moriarty in the ape-like arms of Mort. As she lay swooning, Mort ran a blackened tongue over yellowed teeth and bleeding gums and let forth a lustful sigh. I became alarmed for the damsel's chastity and scooping up the dottle-filled ashtray from my table, hurled it with all my might, striking Mort a mighty wallop to the forehead. The young lady recovered from her swoon, a performance,

I thought, and was off in a flash, whereas Mort went down as if pole-axed.

I already had my two brace in the bag, so forgoing further fishing for the day, I good-naturedly dragged Mort by the feet into the boot of the Bentley and was soon bound for the little cottage hospital in the next village. When we arrived there appeared to be no wheelchair, but by slipping sixpence into the eager grip of Bayleaf, the village gardener, who was working outside, I procured the use of his wheelbarrow to transport a still-unconscious Mort to casualty. On regaining his wit, he became immediately warlike, springing out of the wheelbarrow and advancing with fists clenched. However, a timely right and left across the head with a handy bedpan soon brought the scoundrel to his senses. Recognising my superiority, he doffed a greasy cap and begged we be friends once more. I quickly regretted clasping his reeking carcass to me as I gagged and struggled mightily not to be sick, and strove not to cause offence to my Piscean blood-brother. The stench proved too much, and as my stomach roiled, he pressed my face into the bed-pan, lately used to bludgeon, but now to save my blushes, and I once again thanked the piscatorial deity for the presence of Mort in the world.

The pretty nurse in casualty clipped off the ends of the sutures in Mort's face and nodded at a job well done, whilst his hand began to travel up her shapely thigh, though she proved more than his match, plunging a syringe of morphine directly into his carotid artery. His eyes crossed briefly, and then took on the thousand-yard stare of the shell-shocked infantryman as I lowered him gently into the wheelbarrow and quickly out to the Bentley. We had work to do disposing of the old wooden cross, which the Reverend Farthing had said had been left behind the church.

Evening was falling by the time we repaired to my cosy garden room, and Mort brewed tea as I heated up the game stew for supper. Mixed game, diced streaky bacon, full-bodied red wine, Worcestershire sauce, garlic, juniper berries, crushed cloves, bay leaves and a large dessert spoon of redcurrant jelly for the balance, served with yesterday's toasted bread, seemed a feast fit for a king and we went to it with gusto. Finally, letting forth an echoing, explosive belch, Mort declared himself replete and ready for the hard labour of sawing the cross into manageable sections before getting them back to my workshop for further sectioning into usable lumps for the room heaters of the various kind folk who had already placed orders for the same. Hitching the Bolsover-Sawyer trailer to the Bentley took a mere couple of minutes, and then we were rattling down Main Street and up Church Lane to the unmade road that led round the back of the dark, sepulchral church.

Whilst not a fanciful man, I bowed my head and crossed myself as we entered under the lych-gate, for the churchyard seemed quite menacing at night, and the shadows cast from the floodlights to the front over the various gravestones were unnerving. Mort gasped an oath as he went over and cracked his hip on the corner of a marble angel at prayer, spluttering the question as to why we were here in the middle of the night. For clarity, I tapped his head repeatedly onto an iron urn full of wilted begonias as I explained the importance of the neighbours not seeing me involved in the labour – it would be quite below one's dignity. Mort thanked me for the elucidation and drove his knee forcefully into my groin. We looked hard at one another and silently agreed that the matter, though not closed, was over for the moment.

The oak cross weighed in excess of three hundred pounds, with the upright of ten feet supporting a crossbeam of seven feet. The trailer would not fit through the lych gate, so the plan was to saw the cross into five pieces, carry them between us through the shadowy graveyard to the car, and away back to the cottage. The two-man saw was newly sharpened and made light work of the wood, and we two made half a dozen visits to and from church to trailer and had the wood under a tarpaulin at home before midnight rang from the tower, awakening echoes around the village.

We shared a celebratory tipple of Mort's infamous parsnip liquor before he left for the spinster Arkwright's outhouse – his current address – and I went inside the main house destined to snuggle down next to that rancorous sow upstairs. With a shudder I noticed the moonlight streaming through the intricately-leaded lights that lined the staircase, and knew that with the full moon would come her rising passion, so it was with sick dread that I entered the night-chamber, unsure what fate awaited me.

The next morning as I staggered downstairs, my hair awry and my back in agony, I espied Mort already in residence in the dining room finishing off a plate of kidneys and washing the whole down with a large fresh cup of steaming Java. Leaping up, he beckoned me through the kitchen and into the cold room off the pantry. I lay on the butcher's block as he ripped off my nightshirt and inspected the damage. Sucking air through gapped, rotten teeth, he tutted and left, returning quickly with a steaming bowl of hot salted water with which he bathed the shallow claw marks in my back. I manfully did not cry as astringent was applied, but vowed that one day this torment must end in me culling her, quickly, painlessly, and without cruelty or passion. She merely was what she was: a homicidal maniac.

The pain soon passed after mixing the usual dried willow bark with parsnip wine and in no time I was dressed and striding down the path to help Mort, who stood quite still, with one corner of the tarpaulin raised to inspect the contents of the trailer. The colour had drained from his hideous face, and I followed his gaze to a neat pile of freshly-sawn green oak. Not fifty-year silvered oak but new wood, fresh from the sawmill.

We ran unobserved across Main Street and up the ancient steps into the front of the churchyard carrying the large two-handed saw, and were just as quickly round the back and out of sight of the road. I stood gasping for air as I surveyed the timeworn, venerable cross leaning against the back of the church. Mort grinned, spat onto his hands and began sawing.

The theft of the new cross was investigated with some vigour by Constable Laurel, but his efforts came to naught as the paucity of evidence and witnesses precluded progress and the affair was soon forgotten. A new cross was purchased to be kept under lock and key in one of Farmer Wright's barns. The old cross lies in pieces under some brushwood in the older, unused part of the cemetery, awaiting collection some moonlit night, and Mort and I have made a donation to the church roof appeal to lighten our respective consciences, so all is well. Better than well, for now a thrilling tug shakes me from my reverie as a nice rainbow clears the water as I strike, and battle is joined once again at Star Lake.

CHAPTER FIFTEEN

In Memoriam

Mort wiped a tear from his grizzled countenance as he gazed down at the inscription on the coffin lid five feet below: *Fortiter in re, suaviter in modo* (resolute in action, gentle in manner). He raised a silent prayer to the piscatorial deity that one of our number at Star Lake had been gathered into the good Lord's landing net and been judged good enough to keep. He spat on his hands and began to fill in the grave he had dug for his friend but three days before, for he wanted to attend the wake as soon as possible, most importantly before all the game pie had gone.

Walter Edison, bachelor of this parish, had been the only member other than Mort and myself to stand up to my loathsome wife on the subject of publicising our little water to the world in general. He had duly collected a large swelling or 'mouse' under his left eye, a product of my wife's right hook, but had not gone down to the blow, and for that he was to be applauded. I saw the hag herself stop in front of his likeness above the fireplace in his little Victorian cottage at the bottom of the village near the turning for the Old Great North Road and nod in silent tribute, for she loved a man of backbone and would have no doubt rogered the poor individual had he been alive and fifty years younger. She shot me a dark glance full of menace and then was gone into the crowd, the evil cur Seyton at her heels.

The Reverend Farthing, he that had attended Walter's passing, drifted over for a few words, and I realised with a start that the portly priest was a little drunk. At that moment, Mort appeared in the kitchen doorway, a pewter jack of porter in one hand and a large slice of game pie in the other, waving the latter in an attempt to get my attention. I began to cross the highly-polished parquet flooring, but lost my footing as I slipped on a greasy piece of sausage one of the well-wishers had inadvertently discarded. The daemonhound Seyton naturally laid claim to all things edible on the floor and rushed at the stray *wurst* as if his life depended on it, wrenching my spiteful wife towards the growing conglomeration and also tripping Davies the greengrocer and part-time Sexton, who had his arm on Farthing. We all went down, cannoning into Mort, who showered the potent ale over us.

Later on, as afternoon quietly turned to evening and all the mess had been tidied, Walter's widowed sister Cassandra, with whom he had lived these last twenty years, cleared her throat noisily and had our attention. It appeared he had left but one request in his will, to the effect that he wished a cup to be cast in his name and fished for annually, with a prize of fifty guineas set aside for the winner. The motion was adopted without opposition by all present, who all happened to be members of the syndicate, and a mighty cheer awoke the echoes of the cottage.

I found Mort in the arbour outside, puffing silently on some vile shag that reduced us both to tears and staring thoughtfully into the infinite black velvet night sky. He said nothing, save that he was bothered by the fact that the trophy was to be awarded in open contest, and that anyone might enter for it. With that, he tapped his pipe onto my head in cheerful salute and turned to go. Unfortunately the red-hot dottle took root in my hair, which began to smoulder instantly, and by the time I removed my head from the water butt close by, Mort had gone.

I arose on the day of the Walter Edison Memorial Trophy match feeling sore and out of sorts. In an attempt to ensure the trophy would stay within the confines of our club, the leading piscators, myself of course, Mort, Farmer Wright, Davies, the grocer and sexton, and my noxious wife had embarked on an advanced course of training and conditioning, to ensure we would be at our collective peak when competing for the angling equivalent of the Jules Rimet trophy. This included self-flagellation. The act of hitting oneself with a whip as part of a ritual is known to induce an altered state, heightened awareness and increased physical performance. When she had caught me thus, my wife had snatched the whip out of my hand with a cry of triumph and joy, and had laid about me with all of her not inconsiderable vigour. The sadist would have nearly killed me had it not been for the intervention of Mort, who on hearing my screams, had rushed into the salon to find her towering over my prostrate form. He had taken immediate action and had broken one of the beech chairs over her head and shoulders, stunning her senseless. Seyton had launched himself for Mort's throat, and had been stopped by a savage punch to his chest. Seizing the advantage, Mort grabbed the tyke's tail and hurled him through the open casement to land heavily on the manure heap. The mongrel tried to rise, but collapsed comatose. Then Mort lifted me tenderly and headed for my room in the garden, unfortunately dropping me when he turned to close the shed door behind him. I cared not, for with Mort I was safe, although I knew my wife was quite possibly insane.

He quickly fortified me with a generous libation of parsnip alcohol laced with a thread of methylated spirits. I became aware of the latter as heat blossomed within my chest and I gasped for air, only cooling somewhat as I put the spout of a soda syphon into my mouth and depressed the lever.

That had been the previous week, and since then I had kept my conditioning purely to fishing at Star Lake, and had not spoken at all to the harridan who sat opposite me at the breakfast table contentedly chewing kidneys and tantalising me with brief glimpses of hairy calves and thighs as her knitted negligee rose and fell in syncopation with her heavy breathing. In a conciliatory tone, I suggested discussing tactics for the match which was due to commence in under two hours, but she merely tossed her large head and greasy locks, informing me that she and her ladies would be keeping their own council and would win the trophy, not for the club, but for female piscators throughout the world. With a snort she was gone with Seyton, who turned and bared his teeth as he trotted after his foul mistress.

A shriek from the dull-witted maid, Susan, from the direction of the kitchen marked the arrival of Mort, who was framed in the doorway of the dining room like a nightmare come to life. From reeking trench coat down to boots so rotten one wondered how they stayed round his putrescent feet, he presented a picture of filth and disease, and yet this man was my best friend and the greatest angler known to me. If any could secure the trophy, it would be he, and I told him so as I invited him and his stinking carcass to breakfast.

We loaded up the supercharged Bentley with the tackle and arrived at Star Lake in record time, to be greeted and indeed lauded by the great majority of members who had decided not to fish as they knew they lacked the finer skill possessed by myself and a handful of others. I pitied them, but then realised that the masses had to look up to somebody and if I were he, then so be it, so I raised my hand a little in acceptance of their adulation. I would have liked to pat a small child on the head, but could not find one, so I busied myself putting together my tackle.

There was only one entrant from outside the syndicate, Josiah Hardwick from the Sedgebrook fly fishing club. I had neither seen nor spoken to the rotter since our duel, but was reminded of Mort's words concerning someone from outside taking the prize and felt sick with worry at the awful prospect.

The rules were very straightforward, as there were fewer than a dozen anglers fishing the twenty-one acre lake. The fishing would commence at ten of the clock and finish at two. A maximum of four trout to be taken, the winner being the piscator with the heaviest bag, with contestants fishing wherever they may choose. The Brigadier's ancient little field piece gave forth a bang and a belch of smoke, and the contest was under way. We twelve hurried to different parts of the lake and began fishing.

A rustle from the long grass behind me and a miasma of polluted air around heralded the arrival of Mort, who wheezed none too gently down my ear that he had caught two trout, as had the spinster Arkwright. My wretched wife and Hardwick had one, as had I. I frantically drew in clean air before turning to reply, but found him gone, and again marvelled at his innate ability to move about almost silently.

As the echo from the brigadier's little cannon brought the contest to close, I landed my third to a slowly-fished Wickham's Fancy, and as we gathered for the weigh-in amidst the falling gloom of the late afternoon

I was reasonably confident that the trophy would abide with the club. That happy thought was undone when Hardwick's catch rotated the scales by eleven ounces more than mine. My wife's face was a mask of hate as she realised she was under Hardwick's weight and as she stepped forward, I feared she would strike the man, but she froze as she felt the point of a stiletto in Mort's hand lightly pierce a fleshy buttock. Knowing Mort would not hesitate to push home the blade, she gingerly sidestepped towards her Land Rover, threw in the dog and tackle and roared away in a black haze of diesel exhaust. I sighed and nodded to Mort and turned to Hardwick to begin a congratulatory speech when the squire Elliott, currently conducting the master of ceremonies duties, continued with the final weight contributed by Miss Arkwright.

Thunderous applause greeted the old maid as she strode across the veranda in her suspender waders and rah-rah skirt to receive the trophy from the Reverend Farthing. She had beaten Hardwick by a full nine ounces overall to claim the prize, delighting my wife, no doubt, as they are both vaguely female, pleasing Mort, as they will be able to polish it together, and myself as Hardwick did not win. And, finally pleasing old Walter Edison I think, for as I stood on the first platform from the lodge, his favourite perch, enjoying a pipe of Dutch Niemeyer mixture in the gathering darkness, I felt a chill, frigid wind swirl around me, though the leaves on the nearby trees remained motionless.

CHAPTER SIXTEEN

Fishing in Lilliput

Multum in parvo (much from little)

During his first voyage, Jonathan Swift's Gulliver was washed ashore after a shipwreck to find himself a prisoner of a race of tiny people, less than six inches tall, the inhabitants of the island of Lilliput. That was why Arthur Ransome in his fabulous book *Rod and Line*, published in nineteen twenty-nine, described fishing in small streams as "fishing in Lilliput".

Star Lake is filled by three springs on the lake bed,

constantly pulsing clean, fresh water from the aquifers deep below. In addition she also draws water from the Drover Beck, which chuckles and gurgles its way through fifteen miles of our gorgeous county before emptying finally into the mighty River Trent. Within this rill resides an indigenous population of wild brown trout, the average size six inches in length, with nine inches being a monster indeed. They are imbued with a cunning and extremely keen self-preservation instinct that far outstrips that of the farm-grown trout, and are consequently extremely difficult to catch on an artificial fly, thus making them highly attractive to the piscator, who will pursue them with ardour and then return them gently to fight another day.

Mort and I had already caught our limit of trout for the month from Star Lake, so we determined to have a day on the Beck in pursuit of these smaller kin. As I sat in the ornate green oak porch awaiting his arrival, I cast my mind to planning the day. The tackle of choice must be equally reduced to match the size of the stream, so the rod is no more than five feet, with a size three line at most, as the weight of fish caught will not be a problem, four ounces being the largest I have returned to date.

As I sat there musing, a shadow fell across me and I glanced up into a gorgon's mad eyes. My foul wife was staring intently at me and breathing hard through her large hairy nostrils. I gazed fascinatedly at the large yellow-headed spot on the tip of her crooked nose and ached to squeeze it, but dared not, as I recognised her ire and knew that a precipitous action from myself could well tip her over the edge into insanity.

The previous day I had discovered that she had taken a lover. Not any lover, but the person of Josiah Hardwick, that utter cad and bounder who is the chairman of the Sedgewick Fly Fishing Club. I had done what any other true Englishman would have done and repaired to Hardwick's humble abode to confront the roué about his actions. I ran him to ground in his dingy little shed, to find him tying poor sedge imitations by the light of a greasy flickering paraffin lantern. My lip curled as I observed him finishing the fly not with a double hitch but a single knot. I could take no more, so stripped him, locked his John Thomas in the fly tying vice, and picked up a junior hacksaw from the handy tool rack mounted on the wall. He paled and shook like a man with the plague, begging me not to chop off that which was dear to him. I told him I would never do that, but handed him the saw and told him I was going to set fire to the shed.

His piteous screams haunted me as I left the scene, although I learnt from Mort, who was passing later, that Hardwick had been seen nakedly dousing the flames from the shed and would seem to have been in possession of all his organs at the time, so I regretted my actions not at all. Until now of course, as I faced Nemesis in the form of my own wedded hag who seemed bent on vengeance and violence, the two seeming inseparable to her, accompanied of course, by her evil cur Seyton, whose slavering jaws were now inches from me. But she stayed her hand, her oily, spotty countenance a mask of indecision, and then I realised that if she and her hound attacked, it would be tantamount to an admission of her infidelity. I was deeply interested as the war of emotions raged across her sickly complexion, but really should have not been surprised as her fist whipped up in a vicious uppercut, bereaving me of my senses.

The world stopped spinning, and I found myself staring into the blood-shot eyes of Mort. As he breathed onto me, my bile rose as my stomach roiled at the rotten stench issuing from his poisonous maw, and I again cursed my sensitive proboscis. He retreated a step and told how he had found her and the dog crouched over me as he arrived to accompany me fishing. She told him she had berated me again for not cleaning the shower cubicle after use, and that I had become surly and in need of chastisement. With that, she had departed with the dog. I shook my head again to clear it, thinking myself fortunate to have a wife that could punch with such force, and told Mort to load our tackle for the Beck into the Bentley.

The Beck is nicely fishable for about three miles, from the river just to the east of Star Lake to the boundary wall of the insane asylum, and having parked the Bentley at the outfall, we began to quietly and methodically make our way upstream from pool to pool, short casting with bushy, busy little flies. But by the time we reached the fourth pool, I knew something to be amiss. No dark little shape had shot out even to inspect our offerings. I felt certain I had the glimmering of the answer, for faintly in the mud at the edge of the water was a footprint. I possess an almost uncanny recall, and I had seen that print before, on the night when Mort was attacked at Star Lake by that villain Hardwick.

We covered another two miles of the stream before all tracks or traces disappeared, and as soon as Mort cast a sherry spinner, a fish took the fly and battle commenced. The fight was very short as both pool and trout were small, and in no time, a handsome little brown trout lay snuggled in his large wet paw. Tenderly kissing the brave chap, Mort dipped him gently back into the stream, and he was off under the far bank in a thrice. I looked hard at Mort, who nodded but once before uttering the dread word 'worm'. In a brook such as this, a cleverly-angled small redworm would empty a pool in less than five minutes, as the ravenous fish would lose all caution. My head swam and I felt nauseous as I considered how many years it had taken for the natural stocking of the tributary on which we fished, and how that utter sewer Hardwick could decimate it in a single afternoon. The bounder had attacked my friend, seduced my wife, and most hurtful of all, had set about to ruin the most perfect wild brown fishery in the county. I could take no more and vowed on the spot to cull the rascal with extreme prejudice, even though my freedom might be forfeit. Mort looked at me with bloodshot eyes, nodded once as he patted my shoulder, and led me weeping towards the Bentley and home.

By the time Mort had driven us back to the prettiest cottage in the most pleasant village of the whole county, my mind was settled as to the method of Hardwick's execution. It seemed fitting that one of the oldest sins be punished with an equally ancient weapon: the English longbow, made of yew, six feet in length and etched with the inscription *'Silentum interfectorum' (the silent killer).*

Father's bow, handed down through the generations of our family, would fit the bill very nicely. It took half an hour of diligent searching in the loft to find the oilskin-wrapped package containing the bow, two strings of flax and five thirty-inch arrows of ash, all tipped with deadly military bodkin points. As the shadows lengthened I waited patiently in my garden room for full night, when I would sally forth on my dread errand of retribution.

An owl swooped noiselessly overhead as I parted the primrose bushes surrounding Hardwick's neat, functional little Victorian villa, and my lip curled almost in a snarl as I recognised him framed in the window overlooking the meagre little garden. The darkness of the night contrasted with the lounge light, which silhouetted his skinny frame perfectly for the killing shot, and I grimly nocked an arrow to the string, swinging the bow to the vertical whilst simultaneously drawing the string... which did not move. I increased the force of pull, but neither horn-tipped end of the bow responded to the pressure. The string suddenly snapped, and I feverishly produced the spare, rapidly threaded it over the nocks at either end of the bow and again brought it to bear, peering down the arrow at the scrawny image of Hardwick, who was still standing in the window. Yet try as I might, could bend the bow hardly at all.

Then a hairy paw of a hand ripped the bow from my grasp and I spun to see Mort, clad in a cotton shirt and a sleeveless leather archer's coat. He nocked an arrow with a tube of paper around the shaft, brought up the bow and pulled the string back to his cheek, his muscled forearm quivering with the effort as he brought in excess of one hundred and forty pounds of force to bear on the bow. It responded, bent, and as Mort released the string it propelled the arrow with devastating force into Hardwick's solid oak front door, quivering and making the attached note spin freely around the shaft. He smiled thinly, placed the bow in my hand and was gone before I could utter a word. I shivered as I realised that given a stronger arm, I would have committed cold, callous murder.

The next day, as Mort and I fished Star Lake, chatting as if the night before had never occurred, he informed me of two salient details. Namely that a modern bow draws at approximately sixty pounds pressure and that father's longbow required a hundred and fifty pounds to put a bend in it. I reddened and sought to explain my weakness until he pointed out that the skeletons of longbow archers are recognisably adapted, with enlarged left arms, bone spurs on their left wrists, left shoulders and right fingers, and secondly that Hardwick had fled the village. I asked him what was in the note, to which he replied 'merely good advice' and bade me continue fishing.

CHAPTER SEVENTEEN

The Spring Fair

I sat in the green oak garden room skilfully playing Fernando Sor's Study Number Twenty-Four on my Spanish guitar as the rain streamed down the windows and the gusty winds almost laid the vegetables flat in the garden. Constant heavy rain for the last three days had made a foray to Star Lake unthinkable, and had reminded me painfully of my recent tennis elbow - *Eheu fugaces, labuntur anni* (alas the years slip by). It had left me miserable and tetchy, as Susan, our vacuous and dull daily maid, had learned to her cost this morning. I had sat down to my kidneys at breakfast and had been presented instead with kippers, which I knocked out of her hands, only to see the pair fly through the air, one landing on my foul wife's thick, lank hair, and the other cascading down her ample cleavage, displayed to advantage by her knitted scanty, short nightdress.

Her evil canine companion, who is forever famished, leapt for her heaving, greasy bosom and snatched the offending kipper away, then made a dash for the door. Screaming her fury, the rancorous sow threw the other kipper retrieved from her matted, tangled hair into the departing wake of the dog as the Reverend Farthing entered the dining room. As with any impoverished bachelor clergyman, he too is perpetually famished, so he deftly caught the lightly-smoked fish, slipped it adroitly into a sliced warm roll and popped the same into his maw within a trice. As he sat down I applied my boot to Susan's ample rear to send her rocketing into the kitchen with the accompanying clamour of crashing pans as she collided with most of the contents of the room.

My insane wife was by now all nervous smiles as she curtsied before our august guest, raising one eyebrow provocatively and allowing her scanty attire to rise to reveal a hairy thigh. Farthing, may the saints preserve him, was having none of it and rapped his walking cane hard against her thick skull, bidding her to desist her wanton behaviour. Her eyes flashed defiance as she begged forgiveness, and I felt a momentary fear for the vicar's safety as a growl issued from Seyton, who had returned to his mistress. I need not have worried, for the quick-thinking cleric scooped up the little silver pepper cup from the table and dashed its contents into the face of the cur, who rapidly departed the scene, followed by much sneezing, coughing and canine respiratory distress.

Farthing bade me and the vixen sit as he outlined the purpose of his visit, and had to trap her hand painfully in the table drawer to stop her repeatedly interrupting him. As she sat noisily sucking her fingers, he explained that he was seeking contributions from the more talented and noble members of the community for the church Spring Fair talent contest. I immediately offered a Spanish guitar performance, whilst the beldam at my side indicated she would perform an advanced display of fly casting. He profusely thanked us and had turned to go when my whispered comment to the hag suggesting my performance was superior to hers, resulted in her high-heeled Scholl thudding into my groin. The minister tipped his hat and was through the door as I collapsed writhing on the hand-stitched Moroccan rug, purchased years before on our honeymoon whilst returning from a Tuareg barbecue.

I held the last chord and the echo from that most

beautiful of instruments rang through the room. I started as the door to the garden crashed open under the heavy hobnails of Mort's boot. He begged me to put down the guitar and proceed with all speed to the lake, as he had just been informed by the Moriarty sisters that the Brigadier had hooked 'Old Tom'. I leapt from my seat, smashing my head against a hanging fixture that held half a dozen tea lights and was meant, no doubt, to look twee, and loudly cursed the cow who was forever changing things about the cottage and outbuildings. I ran for the Bentley with Mort in hot pursuit, fervently praying that the old soldier would land the amazing fish.

Generally brown trout have greater longevity than rainbow trout, averaging about five years. In many well-managed fisheries such as Star Lake, some individuals reach ages in excess of 10 years, and it is generally held that Tom was introduced to the lake at a weight of around a pound over a decade ago and would now grace the scales at over eight pounds. Half a dozen of the members claim to have hooked him, but none have ever got him onto the bank. Farmer Wright and Walter Edison (deceased) even got him as far as the landing net, only to lose the battle as he shook his head against the net frame, allowing a fraction of slack line to develop and thus make good his escape.

Therefore Mort and I were hurtling down the dusty lanes to the lake on the rare chance that we might get to see the piscatorial legend on the bank. The supercharger on the Bentley ceased to whine as we turned into the lake's carpark on two wheels and we were out of the car and running past the lodge as the tourer coasted to a halt.

A small crowd was gathered around pontoon number three on the sheep bank and all eyes were focused on the gnarled figure the Brigadier presented as he battled the leviathan that had taken his fly, a Pheasant Tail Nymph, we learned later. My heart was in my mouth, for the man was not young, but he had fought in many conflicts all over the world in his long career as a soldier, so I had every confidence in his ability to win the fight.

After what seemed an age, the fish swirled on the surface and we caught the first glimpse of the enormous brown trout that is Tom. He was magnificent. He dived for the deeps again, pulling as a dog on a lead, but the brigadier held hard and the runs for freedom lessened as Tom lost his strength and went onto his side. Mort was taking no chances at the end of the fight, and grabbing the Brigadier's net, he leapt into the water, where he sank to his thighs, swiftly dipped the net under the fish and staggered out onto the bank.

The piscean giant was beautiful, with a golden belly scattered with black and red spots, and measured twenty-five inches from snout to tail-fork. As Mort raised his hand containing the deadly priest in preparation for sending 'Old Tom' to paradise, he looked to the Brigadier, who quickly shook his head and instead reached into his bag for his camera. He took a dozen photographs of the creature, weighed the fish at eight pounds three ounces and then Mort re-entered the water to gently return the fish, as the Brigadier's arthritic hip would allow no such movement, and with a flick of his massive tail, 'Old Tom' was gone. There was a collective sigh as the fish swam away, which turned into a gasp as it became plain that Mort had discarded both his underpants and trousers before entering the water. As the men looked on in jealousy, the women assembled gazed in awe and longing as he bowed before striding from the water.

The Spring Fair was a roaring success, with visitors from within and outside the parish flocking to support the event, and I grinned broadly as I remembered the highlight of the day, the talent show. Fourteen entries from our village and the neighbouring village down the lane vied in the church hall to be the winner. Refreshments were arranged by the Moriarty sisters with a cracking barbecue supplied by Squire Elliott from the abattoir, and alcoholic drinks from Mort's still. The sideshows, including monkey-in-the-ring and rat-up-a-drainpipe, were particularly popular, and there was a large queue outside the tent of Madame Fontana, an authentic gypsy fortune teller, who bore a striking resemblance to the spinster Miss Arkwright. I saw Mort enter, then leave ten minutes later, red of cheek and blowing hard, and I surmised she must have given him some bad news in his forecast.

The talent contest began promptly at four with Bayleaf the gardener's mimicry, and included items from Fraser of the fish farm, Constable Laurel and Davies the sexton. There cannot be a worse ventriloquist alive, and his performance made my sides ache with laughter. This was followed by my moving contribution on the Spanish guitar and culminated in my very own fishwife's exhibition of casting. What followed almost defied belief, as once again she managed to plumb the depths of tastelessness in an outrageous routine performed merely to shock and outrage the audience. It started out well enough with her roll and steeple casting down the length of the hall as a precursor of things to come. Then a Moriarty sister, the younger, had stepped into the aisle adorned in nothing more than seven silk handkerchiefs, positioned in order to protect her modesty, until my slattern of a wife began systematically removing the kerchiefs with delicately performed false casts. The vicar took a hand, and roaring at the top of his voice, dared any man present to look upon the naked voluptuous woman at the cost of his sight. Whereupon Mort covered half his face with his hand, grinned and whispered that he would risk one eye.

CHAPTER EIGHTEEN

The Threat

The monthly board meeting at Star Lake was in session and becoming interminable. Mort, in his role of fish welfare and stocking manager, was asleep with his head on the table and gently snoring, and I watched fascinatedly as a fly warily flew round his ear as a prelude to landing. I was shocked and repulsed as a fat spider appeared out of Mort's thatch of hair and tried to drag the fly back in to feature on its menu. Luckily, the fly was of sufficient strength and size to resist and buzzed angrily away. Still, it made me ponder what else made its home in or about Mort's stinking carcase.

The Brigadier and Wing Commander were half-heartedly bickering over poacher predation and I longed for the end of the meeting, because when we had entered the lodge, fish had been rising all over the lake and an hour fishing the evening rise would be a perfect end to the day.

The last item up for discussion was sponsored by Todd, the dilatory village postman and secretary of our little club. His proposal was for a Fun Day, primarily aimed at increasing the membership, as some seven places had not been taken up at the start of the season. By inviting family, friends and all-comers to take part in an array of exciting activities, including face-painting, community crafts, fly-fishing workshops and tours of the lake and surrounding fields, this fun-packed day for all the family would raise our profile the little needed to fill the gap in the membership. Entry was to be free, with very modest levies raised on refreshments. Wanting only to be free of the meeting, I raised my hand to second the motion, aware that it would pass unopposed, as the poacher debate never missed a beat and Mort slumbered on.

Cave tacet consentire (beware the silent consent)

The Brigadier brought the meeting to a timely close with a clatter of his gavel onto the table top. I rushed to the lakeside and Mort similarly ran in the direction of the spinster Arkwright's abode, whilst Todd sedately packed his little satchel with the tools of his secretarial trade.

Later that evening as I sat dozing in the garden room with an open copy of *A Fly Fisher's Life*, by the renowned angler Charles Ritz, open on my knees, the door flew open with a crash, propelled by Mort's hobnailed boot. The owner of the boot leapt inside, and brandishing a grotesque fist under my noble nose, asked what I proposed to do about the situation.

I am a charming man of equitable temper, but I will not be spoken to thus by one of inferior breeding such as this hooligan, who was doubtless born at low tide in the gene pool. Throwing my book to one side, I leapt to my feet, assuming an Nguni war stance, and brought my foot, ensconced in a delightful velvet Persian slipper, hard up under Mort's chin, snapping his head backwards and catapulting his lower dentures through the open door of the log burner. With a cry, he approached the fire with hands outstretched and succeeded in retrieving the errant teeth, now black with soot, and crammed them back into his mouth. He shrieked as the vulcanite, a form of hardened rubber into which the porcelain teeth were set, seared his empty gums. In this century, acrylic resin and other plastics are now used, but Mort was a traditionalist, and had inherited the teeth from his father.

I immediately forgave him his caddishness and grabbed the soda siphon from the ornate occasional table, quickly directing a cooling jet of the soft drink into his mouth. He grinned and nodded his thanks as I roared with laughter to see a row of black teeth upon a row of white in his ugly maw.

After begging my forgiveness for the manner of his entry, he launched into an explanation of what was vexing him so. Roger, the garrulous and chatty windbag who is also landlord of the Broad Oak, our village pub, had eavesdropped upon a private conversation between Secretary Todd and a half-dozen surly-looking coves in the snug of the aforementioned hostelry. Mort then explained the consequences of the words that had been overheard. All six scoundrels were related to the secretary, and when they obtained membership of our club, the blackguards intended to insinuate themselves eventually to the board, thus giving control one day to Todd. He intended to present them to various members over the course of the Fun Day, when guards would be lowered and suspicions of strangers less likely to take root, in preparation for them gaining membership to the club.

The thought of that dullard, that rapscallion, leading our merry band of piscators left me numb with worry and trembling with anger. I decided there and then that he must be culled, slowly and painfully. Mort agreed he must be stopped, but not by murder, as he would not see me, his benefactor, subjected to incarceration upon arrest. He bade me leave things to him and all would be well, and I thanked all the fishing deities once again for the presence of such a man as he.

The morning broke bright and fresh for the Fun Day, although I awoke feeling somewhat testy after rather a bad night. The hag had gone up to bed first as I had tarried to finish a chapter of that Skues classic *Minor Tactics of the Chalk Stream*, and with some trepidation I had peered around the bedroom door to see her sprawled naked on the king-size mattress gorging on a large jar of mixed pickles in vinegar. Startled, she had looked up and seen me in the doorway, longing warring with revulsion etched upon my fine features. She rose from the bed and moving soundlessly on her large hairy feet, pulled me sinuously from the portal and into the bed, lost in lust and loathing in equal measure. Next morning as we breakfasted on kidneys and bacon, washed down with copious amounts of Grumpy Mule coffee, I considered my fortune at being wedded to the creature and idly wondered what plan Mort had up his sleeve for later in the day down at Star Lake.

At ten of the clock, the seductress and I pottered down to the lake in the Bentley. I had not seen Mort since the night before, as he was still staying in spinster Arkwright's outhouse, yet felt quite content, as Mort was never so effective as when he was unseen, and moreover, he had never yet let me down. I shivered in a frisson of pleasure, though whether in anticipation of Todd's downfall or my wife's serpentine tongue that was languidly licking my face, I do not know.

Polite applause from the small crowd assembled in front of the lodge greeted Todd as he jauntily climbed the few stairs in order to address the gathering. Most of the members were there, as were many visitors, including the relatives Todd wished to insinuate into the membership. My hackles raised immediately as he welcomed people to *his* club and went on to hope that *his* Fun Day would be a success, and I was pleased that I had hidden father's small hunting arbalest complete with quarrels in one of the dustbins to the rear of the lodge, as I knew I would have to cull the dullard should Mort fail in his attempts to ruin the day.

An unknown voice from the crowd asked if he had ever thought of higher office at the club, causing a few of the older members to bristle where they stood, and as he opened his mouth to reply, there came a rending sound and Todd disappeared through the floor in a shower of sawdust, to the accompaniment of much laughter and guffawing from the spectators. His cronies rushed to the hole to help him out, and facing the assembly with something of a rictus grin, Todd declared the day officially open.

On reflection, I really did feel for Todd. To go against Mort was to confront a force of nature, so father's arbalest was returned unused to Steeple Cottage, to reside next to all his other weapons, whilst Todd was humbled and chastened, confounded and confused, deflated and overcome, all by means he was never aware of.

It would remain a mystery as to how a little caustic soda was introduced into the face paint, causing blotches and irritation. Similarly how the Brigadier would get impaled in the ear by a large fly as Todd tried to show off his casting technique. The enigma of how the tour of the lake and surrounding fields stumbled across the upturned hornet's nest, and why the barbecue run by one of Todd's relatives blew up so spectacularly, remain to be explained.

The club enrolled no new members that day, as Todd and his cohorts were marched into the woods by my wife and the female members. It would appear the women became aware of the nefarious plot and exacted a vengeance only a woman would countenance upon a man. Either way, Todd was absent from the lake and the next quarterly meeting and would never again meet my wife's eyes when delivering either parcel or letter to the house. Mort however, would have none of it, and roared and hooted as we shared a glass of his potent parsnip liqueur in the garden room. He told me how he had entered the woods after the ladies and had discovered seven pairs of pants and trousers hanging from the trees in flames. The men stood dejected and huddled whilst the harpies jeered and took photographs.

CHAPTER NINETEEN

Taking the Lead

The Reverend Farthing was on his knees, with hands clasped and head thrown back. A beatific smile graced his features as the Holy Spirit suffused him with joy. The first drops of rain to fall on his forehead made him start and raise his eyes to the church roof, eyes that narrowed as he perceived daylight through the timbers. Rays of light that should have been blocked by the intervening lead streamed through as shafts of the purest ambience as they illuminated the swirling dust motes. Fury now swam over the Reverend's patrician features as he realised that thieves had once again stripped the lead off the roof of the church, and rising, he quickly left in search of that bastion of the law, Constable Laurel.

The police officer belched softly as he finished his early lunch of sage sausages and onions and regarded the curate through eyes with four decades' experience of assaying both criminal and victim. This experience had bestowed upon him the ability to simultaneously calculate the odds of solving a particular crime whilst assessing what a potential victim would accept as a reasonable effort invested by the constabulary. The answer that blossomed in his consciousness was a respectable forty-one percent chance of catching the culprit with a seven-hour investment of official police time. Rising and wiping his mouth with the crisp cotton napkin, he assured the cleric all would be well and ushered him out of the Police House, whilst mentally gauging the whereabouts of a certain gentleman of the parish, Mortimer Sykes.

Lead is a chemical element in the carbon group, known by the symbol Pb from the Latin *plumbum*. It is a soft, malleable and heavy metal, with a bluish-white colour after being freshly cut which soon tarnishes to a dull grey when exposed to air. It is widely used in building construction and weights, and extensively in the manufacture of bullets. This last fact caused the good copper to put Mort as the chief suspect in the investigation, as he was a well-known purveyor of illegal game, and as such would use large quantities of the stolen metal in the latter activity. So, in short time and with a light heart, he pointed the official police cycle in the direction of Star Lake and slowly pedalled off into the warmth of the afternoon. He knew Mort favoured a session with the trout before lunch, followed by a nap on the veranda of the fishing lodge – *scio te inimicus* (know thine enemy) – and as old habits indeed do die hard, Laurel was certain Mort was still unaware of the difference between mine and thine when it came to rabbits, pheasants and the weatherproofing of God's house.

He trundled down the unmade lane, onto the fishery and past the signing-in shed, to be met by the fabulous vista of Star Lake as he leaned the cycle against the low veranda railings. As usual, the sight of the water almost took his breath away as he cast about in search of Mort. A light, warm wind was blowing gently from the south-east and the intermittent swirls of rising fish gorging themselves upon a large hatch of buzzers almost made him giddy. He physically ached to have a rod in his pudgy fist.

For a moment he was tempted to throw off his official tunic, grab one of the spare rods perpetually set up in the rack and rush to the water's edge to pursue the atavistic urge that threatened to overwhelm him. However, common sense prevailed and with a shiver, he was mentally back to the stolid and solid presence of the law. A Moriarty sister, the looker, was sweeping the short flight of stairs and nodded to the lodge door in response to Laurel's enquiry. Then she turned, shook her head and smiled as she continued with her work and wondered what Mort had been up to this time.

She jumped and ejaculated an oath as Mort crashed through the picture window head first and onto the veranda in a forward roll. He was up quickly and lightly onto the balls of his feet as Laurel emerged through the door, his truncheon in his hand and determination writ large across his fat face. Mort rushed in with fists flailing, but Laurel had been a brawler first and copper second and reacted instinctively by going for throat and groin, and with boot to one and stick to the other had Mort *hors de combat* within seconds. He knelt on aching knees next to the prostrate man and tapped him none too gently on the forehead with his official hardwood club, suggesting that if the lead were to be returned by dawn tomorrow, further unpleasantness could be avoided, for he could prove nothing, short of a full confession from Mort, which both men knew would not be forthcoming. However, such is the bond between piscators that later that afternoon both men were fishing the rise on the far sheep bank, laughing together at some joke or remembered tale.

I was preparing a late, lone supper as Mort staggered into the kitchen, obviously still in pain from his battered gonads, although the bruising around his throat had already started to subside. He flung a large freshly-shot hare onto the table before collapsing into the scrubbed pine chair. I decided to jug the hare and proceeded to cut it into pieces and cook it with red wine and juniper berries in a tall jug stood in a pan of water. As this dish is traditionally served with the hare's blood and port wine, I added both at the end of the cooking process for a rich, ruby-red gravy, which we mopped up with freshly-baked garlic bread.

Mort belched loudly and stridently and declared himself full. Retrieving his hip flask from reeking trousers, we toasted, and as the fire from his distilled parsnip wine blossomed painfully in my chest we fell to discussing his precarious predicament with the law. That he had stolen the lead was not in question, but I was unable to understand why, until he told me he was owed money by the church for digging five graves over the last six months, and the lout, rather than approach Farthing or Davies the sexton, had taken payment in kind.

I looked malevolently at the cretin and unable to control myself any longer, I unleashed an uppercut that lifted the wretch from the chair and onto his back. However, my superior nature intervened immediately and I gently cradled his bloodied head and whispered all would be well, as this time Mort was relying on me to pull the irons from the fire, rather than the other way round. With Mort having been the senior partner for so long, as it were, in disaster recovery, I hoped I would finally find my feet and save the day, whilst my older companion, somewhat reluctantly I fancied, would relinquish power and authority to the younger, stronger, buck. As he drifted into retirement I fancied he would look kindly upon his usurper as a saviour, and perhaps under different circumstances, the son he never had.

All this wool-gathering ceased as Mort savagely twisted my nose and asked what we were going to do about Constable Laurel and the lead, as on the morrow he would expect the metal to have been returned. I decided upon two courses of action. As the lead from the church could have Mort's fingerprints on it, I proposed we should hide it, since it was one thing for the law to suspect him and quite another to have the proof to convict my dearest friend and obtain a custodial sentence for him. Then we would obtain new lead, and leave it anonymously outside the church, satisfying all parties. We would sell the original lead after a period of time and not be too badly out of pocket.

Mort somewhat ashamedly took me to the rear of Miss Arkwright's outhouse, where he was temporarily lodging, and with a flourish removed a tarpaulin to reveal a pile of sheet lead, glimmering dully in the moonlight. Silently we transferred it to the Bolsover-Sawyer trailer attached to the Bentley and quietly made our way to Star Lake, the motor burbling away at little more than a tick-over, arriving at the bay where the two rowing boats were moored within twenty minutes. I had decided, upon reflection, that selling it was too risky a proposition, even after an interval of time had passed, as detection for the crime would surely follow, so I had decided to bury it forever, as it were. The lead was much heavier than either of us expected, and the water was almost level with the gunwales as we gentry rowed to the middle of the lake, but it made hardly a splash as we consigned the load of heavy metal to the deep.

The second part of my plan was made all the easier as Mort had already spoken to an acquaintance upon the matter of leaving a fresh pile of lead on the vicarage green by daybreak, and as we contentedly puttered back towards the village, it was decided that I would sleep on Mort's bed and he on the floor at the good spinster's abode, so as not to disturb my frightful wife's sleep.

I awoke the next morning to the sound of heavy rain hammering noisily onto the corrugated tin roof of Mort's quarters and clutched my temples with the palms of my hands as I tried unsuccessfully to quell the incessant pain and hammering in my head, caused by incautiously imbibing Mort's latest batch of home-made sloe gin the night before as we had toasted my first successful tilt at the righting of wrongs. The door creaked open as Mort entered, dressed in revoltingly stained underpants and hobnailed boots, a copy of *The Times* held to protect his filthy, shaggy hair from the rain and a steaming cup of fresh nettle and powdered willow bark tisane for my headache.

An hour and one of Miss Arkwright's famous black pudding and egg muffins later, Mort and I were returning to Steeple Cottage in the still teeming rain. As we purred through the village in the Bentley, I noted with pride that some workmen were already transporting lead from the pile on the vicarage green up to the church. I had not realised how easy it could be to overcome the difficulties that life throws at us, and mentally admonished myself for according Mort too much credit for doing so in the past.

As we entered my gravelled drive I noted Clarke the builder's van and wondered what he had come to do. Running through the rain, I came to a halt inside the elaborate porch, Mort cannoning into my back as I stared into the lobby. The hag and bane of my life was talking to the builder in her coat and galoshes, with umbrella raised, inside the house, surrounded by pots and pans on the floor catching the falling drops of water, and demanding of the bewildered builder that he repair the badly leaking roof immediately. I opened my mouth but said nothing as Mort dragged me outside by my coat-tails, propelled me into the Bentley and turned her in the direction of the lake. When asked whence we were going, he grinned, winked and reminded me that we knew where to get some lead, as mine had obviously been stolen during the night.

CHAPTER TWENTY

Poor Relations

I sat in the panelled study after breakfast and studied once more the letter which had been delivered that morning by the dullard postman Todd. I surmised that he had reverted to his old habit of steaming open certain letters of mine, as the sealed flap was a little concertinaed, a sure sign that the envelope had been tampered with. I was a little surprised, as I thought I had cured him of this peculiar habit some months ago, when Mort had come up with the idea of sending me a primed rat-trap in the post. Sure enough, Todd had arrived at the cottage carrying a parcel, with his fingers heavily bandaged. I had managed to squeeze his injuries hard as he passed over the package and the message was silently accepted that I knew what he had been up to. As I turned the envelope, the return address gave the answer as to why Todd had reverted to type on this occasion. The missive was from Sedgebrook Fly-fishing Club.

I had not thought of our poorer fishing neighbours since the craven departure in the night of their chairman, Hardwick, some months earlier, so I was surprised to hear from them as our natural ties were non-existent, due to the gulf in class not only in the fishing but of the membership in general. Their club tended to attract the less well-educated and sportsmanlike angler, whereas Star Lake seemed to attract the acme, the ultimate piscators, in short, gentlemen fishermen and women. However, as I am a philanthropist by nature, I decided I would read their tatty little missive.

The first paragraph was filled with obsequious and submissive ramblings, an abject and fawning description of the hard times they came to find themselves in. It appeared that when Hardwick had fled he had taken a fair amount of the club's meagre capital, leaving it on the point of collapse, and without an immediate cash injection, the club would fold. I am not a hard man, but fair of nature and outlook, and would not see fellow piscators in undue hardship, so with great fortitude and patience, I read to the end of the document, finishing with a slight trembling in my hands as an idea began to take root in my great intellect. Just then a shout from outside, followed by low, sultry laughter, brought me to my senses and led me towards the French windows and the patio beyond. On reaching the threshold, I perceived a sight that made my blood run both hot and cold, although on future nights when sleep evaded me the memory of it would also bring a smile to my handsome features.

The hot august sun beat down out of a cloudless, blue sky as the two people on the terrace made the most of the recent clement weather. My foul wife disported herself on a rusty old sunbed, clad in a revealing knitted swimsuit in the disruptive pattern camouflage of the British armed forces, whilst rubbing in a sunscreen lotion which I presumed to be from the rendered fat of a fresh corpse, as I had observed her the previous evening poring over her book of spells. However, on closer inspection, it was from the Timothy White's suncare range of products, so I was somewhat relieved, until I turned my attention to Mort. He too was sunning himself lying face-down on the Yorkshire slabs, attired in a filthy thong of dubious origin. The cur Seyton wandered in from the garden, and padding over to the recumbent Mort, sniffed his bottom.

Startled by the sudden frigid moist intrusion into his buttocks, Mort passed wind mightily, the force of the gust inflating the thong slightly. The unfortunate hound inhaled deeply. It tried to turn and run, but managed only a couple of toppling steps before collapsing in an insensible heap. Mort threw back his head and roared with laughter and the hag beside him cackled insanely, running sharp nails freshly painted with Hammerite down his spotty, greasy back, which drew blood. I coughed loudly to interrupt the tableau and Mort looked away embarrassed, whilst the siren merely shrugged and continued to read the copy of *Period Homes* she had plucked from the large pile of quality magazines piled next to her. I again thought how a woman could be so like a wheelbarrow; so hard to push, yet so easy to upset.

Scarcely able to contain my excitement, I gestured Mort to follow me through the house and out to the green oak garden room. Passing through the house, he had collected a throw from one of the sofas and had hastily wrapped it around himself so that he looked like some grotesque version of Mahatma Gandhi conjured from a drug-fuelled session of opiates or worse. I bade him sit as I put a taper to the little methylated spirit stove and popped on a kettle filled with fresh spring water in preparation for a pot of Oolong, the finest of teas. The taste varies widely, from sweet and fruity with honey aromas to woody and thick with roasted aromas depending on the style of production. Mort however did not possess my delicate palette, preferring the tea from the village stores. He produced a crumpled teabag from his soiled thong and tossed it casually into his favourite chipped mug.

We both lit pipes, his a foul, acrid-smelling shag clashing with my light aromatic Niemeyer mixture, with Black Cavendish, Burley, Cavendish and Kentucky tobaccos, to name but a few of the fourteen included in every glorious ounce. I opened the small vent in the roof, and as the smoke cleared a little and I was able to discern the ugly visage of my greatest friend, I outlined my newly-formed plan. In essence it was absurdly simple. In practice there might be some minor problems, but overall, I believed that acquiring Sedgewood Lake for our ladies, banning them furthermore from Star Lake, which would become the preserve of the men, was a sound policy for a brilliant piscatorial future for all members.

Mort sucked his teeth and tapped his foot, beating a tattoo upon the floor as he thought over my brilliant plan. Grasping my ears, he delivered a savage head-butt, the like I have been on the receiving end once only when my wife had discovered me and Elsie Partridge, our one-time cook, upon the table in the cool-room off the kitchen. Stars danced wildly before my eyes as Mort delivered the coup-de-grace with a stunning straight left, quickly rendering me unconscious.

At last the room stopped spinning and I regained enough of my faculties to sit up and grin. I found myself on the stone table in the cool-room, aware of the irony of my surroundings. Mort, who had been squatting on the stool in the corner, stood up and advanced with huge fists clenched, but they were instantly lowered as I met him in peace with arms outstretched and brought my boot up sharply into his groin. With a strangled squeak, he fell into my arms and with honour satisfied we sat on the ancient oak settle just inside the kitchen. I was puzzled as to his assault, but forgave him instantly as he laid certain events out before me.

On his way to the spinster Arkwright's house the previous evening, he had espied lights through the primrose bushes that surround Hardwicke's demesne. Curiosity piqued him, as the place had been unoccupied for some weeks, so he had approached the shabby house and stuck a greasy ear to the window pane of the dining room. Hardwicke and his poisonous wife, Lettuce, were deep in conversation and in a potted version, Mort told me of their plan for Sedgebrook Lake. Hardwicke had surmised, correctly, that I would make a bid for their lake and club. He would let this happen, but and then he intended to do all within his power to wreck the enterprise, including poisoning the fish and burning the Sedgebrook fishing lodge – in actuality little more than a large shed – to the ground.

I rose quivering with rage, but Mort slammed me back onto the settle, saying that there was more. Hardwick also intended a secret campaign against Star Lake herself, and would not cease until I was ruined as the leading light of our happy little fraternity.

There and then, I decided to cull the cad. The bounder, it seemed, would never leave me or mine alone. I would put my affairs in order over the next few days, confront the scoundrel and blow out his brains with my shotgun before surrendering myself to Constable Laurel for justice to be done. Mort however was, as usual, one step ahead of me - *Res plus valet quam verba* (actions speak louder than words).

That very night as I lay upon the billiard table in a Mort-induced drunken stupor, he took himself to Hardwick's little Victorian villa and kicked open the front door with one swing of his great hobnailed boot. He found Josiah and Lettuce making love before a roaring log fire. Grabbing Lettuce by her sweaty locks, he quickly stunned her with a small stroke of his lead-filled salmon priest. Josiah had attempted to crawl into the hall, until he froze at the sound of Mort cocking his single barrel poacher's shotgun and Josiah was overwhelmed with blackness as my friend sharply brought the stock of the weapon crashing down onto the back of his head. He awoke nauseous and dizzy, naked and unable to move. He shifted his head to the left and right, and found Mort had tied him to the railway track that borders Star Lake and was quietly sitting opposite, patiently puffing on a pipeful of malodorous shag. A faint whistle echoed in the distance and a tingle was felt in the rails. Hardwicke released his bowels and Mort's face split in a huge grin.

The former residence of the Hardwicke couple was sold just three weeks after the 'FOR SALE' board went up, and is now home to a charming young couple from the city, her slightly swollen abdomen mute testimony to an addition to the family soon. Mort had disappeared from the locale for some weeks after a weeping and soiled Hardwicke was temporarily admitted to the asylum. After a short stay he had departed the parish with his obnoxious Lettuce a broken man, and never to return.

I would like to report a happy ending for Sedgebrook Lake, but I can merely say that the imbecile Todd, our recalcitrant postman, has taken ownership of the said water. I would wish him well, although in truth I feel that 'something wicked this way comes'. But that is something for tomorrow, or the day after, for the sun is shining down at Star Lake, the fish are moving, and I have just missed a take, that most thrilling moment when for a second you and the trout are connected as one.

CHAPTER TWENTY-ONE

Working Party

When our piscatorial society was formed it was agreed that we should have as few rules as possible, and to that end, only seventeen are observed. Number five states that all able-bodied members must give two days' labour per season at the lake devoted to maintenance of the environs, under the direction of the committee. Mort and I had put our names down for one of the pre-planned working parties, and on a fine spring day we lined up with Bayleaf the gardener, Farmer Wright, Fraser from the fish farm and Davies the greengrocer and part-time sexton in front of the

Wing Commander for a tool inspection and briefing of the day's planned work.

There was an exquisite aroma of frying flitch from the lodge as the Moriarty sisters prepared the traditional breakfast fare of bacon sandwiches and hot sweet tea to fortify our attempts against the physical labour we were all so unused to, and having passed muster with the pre-work inspection, we set to the fare with hearty appetites. Mort belched softly, counting himself full, and once again ran his calloused fingers up under the hem of Miss Moriarty the younger's micro-miniskirt, lingering briefly to caress the varicose veins thereon, before we set out for the sheep bank. Our day's task was excavating a recess in the clay for the construction of an additional fishing platform, whilst the others headed for the trees to commence pollarding activities. These ten-foot piers give piscators safe access to the lake from the steep, uneven banks and are but one more indicator of the quality both of the water and its administration.

Mort stripped to baggy, stained underpants, leapt into the shallow water and commenced digging, whilst I attacked the earth from above, and our shovels became a blur as the sods flew onto an increasing pile behind me. At midday Miss Moriarty the elder appeared, bearing mature cheddar sandwiches and a flask of tea. Mort was out of the water in a flash and began a series of exercises or *Katas*, the Japanese martial art movement with stepping and turning, while attempting to maintain perfect form in an attempt to impress the trollop carrying the refreshments. With hand over mouth she watched Mort as he went through his entire repertoire, including the Eagle, the Hare and finally the Scorpion. All went well until half-way through the Praying Mantis, when, just as Mort's arms were raised in the attack pose, the elastic in his underpants finally succumbed and snapped. His prodigious member rolled out of confinement almost down to his knee, and Mistress Moriarty screamed and fled for the safety of the lodge. Mort chuckled as he restored the errant briefs and I tossed him a bungee cord to cinch around his waist before we sat down to eat before recommencing the digging.

A dull metallic ringing and a pain up my arm as the spade stopped indicated an obstacle buried in the earth. Further probing with the shovel revealed it to be of some size, so I bade Mort attack the ground with vigour from the water side as it were, so we might reveal what the blockage was. He soon struck metal and uncovered one end of the mystery, which appeared to be round and possibly two feet in diameter, lying horizontally under perhaps three feet of loam.

As we uncovered more of the object from above, I was struck by the similarity between it and the large hot water tank in the airing cupboard back at the cottage; in fact the round cover plate half-way up looked as though it was there to accept a heating element. As we stood in contemplation with hands resting on spade handles, the Wing Commander arrived, red of cheek and short of wind, to reprimand Mort for exposing himself so foully in the face of the impressionable Moriarty, but then stopped open-mouthed as he stared at what we had exposed. He bade us not to panic but to walk quietly away to a distance of at least a thousand yards. I opened my mouth to speak, but was moved to silence by the steely determination that was radiating from the old combatant as he glared like the fabled basilisk at the object in the earth. Through clenched teeth and in little more than a whisper, he informed us we had uncovered a German parachute mine, or *Luftmine*.

With shaking limbs we turned and hurried away towards the lodge, which was less than a thousand yards away, but only a little. A drizzle had started and no one wanted to get wet, and we thought the prospect of tea and dry surroundings cancelled out the slim chance of getting injured because we had failed to withdraw a few yards further. The other chaps had returned to the lodge and Farmer Wright set off at a trot across the fields to the nearest village to telephone the authorities, whilst Bayleaf and Fraser stationed themselves at the other end of the track at the entrance to our corner of our piscatorial world to stop anyone entering.

Davies paced up and down whilst the Wing Commander outlined our predicament. He told us that the Luftmine was a naval mine dropped from an aircraft. Well over two thousand pounds in weight and over eight feet long, it was constructed of aluminium and detonated by impact or by disruption to the magnetic field generated inside. They were deadly, as the blast could kill for a thousand yards; the famous singer Al Bowlly was killed by one exploding outside his flat in Jermyn Street, London, during the Blitz. Accordingly the Wing Commander cautioned us again about remaining, but nodded in approbation when none moved. I believed I was being brave and the rest were merely following my noble stance.

Footsteps outside announced the return of Farmer Wright, who literally fell through the door gasping for breath. He told us the bomb disposal group was on its way and would be there within the hour. Both sisters tottered towards the kitchen on impossibly high heels to put the kettle on.

Lente hora, celeriter anni (the years fly, the hours drag)

Yes the years go by quickly, but this hour passed as

slowly as if on leaden legs, until finally we heard an engine note from outside the lodge and Mort rushed in from his vigil to confirm the arrival of the RAF bomb disposal group. A fat major wearing the laurel and inverted bomb badge of his calling strode confidently in carrying a black doctor's bag and demanded to know where the 'patient' was. The two accompanying corporals beamed at us and demanded tea, while the Moriarty sisters practically drooled onto the threadbare carpet, immovable and trancelike as they stared at the smart servicemen. Mort soon got them going with a sharp kick up each rump with a hobnail boot, and they departed screaming for the kitchen.

The major would only accept directions to the bomb, and refused to be led, so the three of them swiftly departed in a long-wheelbase Land Rover and we turned back into the lodge. The sisters had thoughtfully provided sausage sandwiches followed by jelly and trifle to keep our spirits up, but I had little appetite as at every moment I was expecting to hear a dull roar and feel the shock wave as the German device obliterated all traces of three brave men in an instant. Mort thanked the girls by leering down their collective cleavages and running a moist tongue repeatedly over his thick, sensuous lips.

An hour passed, then two, and the light in the west began to dim as the sun sank exhaustedly to its bed.

We heard footsteps on the wooden boards and the door flew open as the three saviours stepped smartly in. The major explained that it was an old one thousand kilogram *Luftmine B*, fitted with a standard magnetic fuse. There were no booby-traps and no complications and as we spoke they were carrying out trepanation, in which a hole is cut into the side wall of the bomb and the explosive mixture extracted through a combination of steam and acid liquification. In another hour, all that would remain would be the enormous aluminium casing, which would be removed by a government contractor, as that amount of scrap was worth a considerable sum.

Mort opened his mouth to speak, thought better of it and quietly left the lodge. The sisters began their swooning again, and telephone numbers were exchanged before the trio disappeared again into the night, promising to return in the morning to give the final all-clear. I decided to stay on site as the hour was late, and goodness only knew what would happen should I awake the trollop at home, for tonight was a full moon, the madness and lust would be upon her, and I shuddered to imagine the foulness she would sink to should I appear in her bed. I set up a camp bed on the veranda, for the night was not cold, and lay there listening awhile to the night birds, the odd fish rising and the wind in the willows, struggling with the conundrum of why only ladies from earth won the Miss Universe title.

I awoke from a shallow sleep as the bomb disposal team arrived and we made our way to the site of the mine. The trepanation used to make the device inert had evidently done its work, as a large pancake of filthy-looking suds stained a wide area of grass. This goo was perfectly harmless, the major had explained on our way out, and would rapidly biodegrade after further dilution through natural rainfall. What rendered us speechless however, was the disappearance of the casing. The mystery deepened when it was learned that Bayleaf and Fraser had remained all night at the gate against intrusion, so the scrap had not left by road.

I turned away and grinned as he barked orders to the corporals. All day they searched for the casing. Mort appeared in the afternoon and sat on the lodge steps in the sunlight cutting his horny toenails with a vicious cut-throat razor, humming a ditty I was sure I knew. Later when I whistled it to my cow of a wife the penny dropped when she identified it as a song written by Arthur J. Lamb and composed by Henry W. Petrie in 1897, entitled *Asleep in the Deep*.

CHAPTER TWENTY-TWO

Last Day of the Season

Winter will come early this year I think. The condensation that mists and beads the bedroom windows come daybreak was on the verge of freezing this morning, and only half way through October I was already longing for the spring. The last day of October marks the end of trout fishing at Star Lake, but an extension of a month granted by the owners meant we fished that year until November's end. With Christmas in the shops at that time, it does not feel right to be in pursuit of the lovely trout beyond then.

Mort and I planned to have an outing to the lake

that day before returning to the Broad Oak for a libation and an early supper with Roger, the genial host. That ugly trollop I am married to was attacking her grilled kidneys with gusto at the breakfast table as Seyton the cur looked with longing eyes at every forkful she crammed into her gash of a mouth. A photographer was due to arrive mid-morning to take a series of shots of the awful beldam for a forthcoming feature devoted to lady anglers in the *Trout Fisher's Life* magazine, and for a week she had been primping and fettling herself until every tube of ghastly cream and lotion in the house had become exhausted.

I sighed as she outlined how this could be the opportunity for improving the standing and public profile of our most charming little water as she had done so many times in the past, and then I made the cardinal sin of trying to interrupt her mid-flow. Now she would punish me, by reminding me who had complete control and power over whom. She pushed the cleared breakfast plate away and rising, languidly stretched her long simian arms above her head, exposing thick matted tufts of underarm hair. The morning sunlight poured through her coarsely-knitted nightdress, accentuating her muscly torso, and I groaned in reluctant longing. Seyton growled warningly as he detected the pheromones and testosterone and rose to pad around the room, anxiously glancing between us, not understanding the primal forces at work within the room. He howled and tried to bite me, but I grabbed both his tail and ruff and hurled him through the open window and into the ornamental pond, quickly cutting off the protesting barking as I slammed and secured the window. Turning, I went to grab her in my arms, just as the door flew open to crash against the wall under the propulsion of a large hob-nailed boot. Mort had arrived in full fishing gear ready for our trip. I glanced from him to her, edging for the door in answer to the call from the lake. Her bloodshot eyes narrowed and her fist shot out to catch me a shocking blow to the cheek, but as the second blow arced towards me, Mort grabbed her tightly by the wrist, saving my features from further damage. He squeezed until tears sprang to her eyes, nodded once and let her go, then turned for the door, oblivious to the naked hatred pouring forth from the woman.

As we crossed the threshold, there was a patter of paws on the gravel accompanied by a vicious growl as my wife's dripping hound launched himself for my throat. Mort caught him by the tail in mid-flight and spun on his heel like a hammer thrower, launching the dog into the air to land heavily on the nearby compost heap, where it lay in a panting pile. Brushing an imaginary hair from my classically-cut tweed we climbed into the Bentley, primed her with a good dash of high octane juice and seconds later we were hurtling down the lane towards the lake with the supercharger keening lustily, blithely ignorant of the wronged woman in our wake.

The Brigadier glanced up from his fly-tying vice set up on the veranda of the lodge, where he was finishing a daddy-long legs or crane fly, a creature which is irresistible to trout as they skip and trip across the surface of the water, and nodded at us as we arrived. The Moriarty sisters peeked out from the kitchen, lightly dusted in flour from their baking, and coloured up immediately as Mort bowed and blew them a kiss. I glanced across the lake, recognising Farmer Wright working the distant railway bank as Squire Elliott from the slaughterhouse attempted his magic in the near corner. Doctor Bell and Clarke the builder were recognisable, as were Sexton Davies and Fraser from the fish farm. All good, competent anglers, but blank and fishless thus far according to Vasilles, our tackle shop owner, who was lingering near the kitchen and hoping for a conversation, or more, with either of the good sisters. This indicated a difficult time lay ahead for Mort and me on the water.

Three hours later, a dozen anglers with nary a fish between them trudged off the water shaking their heads. The flat calm, gin-clear and lifeless lake had reduced these doughty piscators to questioning whether the water had been cleared by poachers, until Mort calmly strode into the lodge and laid two fat rainbow trout onto the plain deal table. He held up his hand to forestall questions, stating that red buzzers had caught the fish, and left to gut them in the old Belfast sink outside. I think at that moment that I was most proud to be Mort's friend and confidant.

The sisters went to put the kettle on, whilst Roger announced that if he could have the trout, he'd get his chef Gaston to make one of his famous creamy trout and asparagus risottos up at the Broad Oak tonight. Mort shouted agreement through the open window, and as the tea appeared, I stepped out onto the veranda to share a pipe with him. The light had all but gone and the moon was low, large and red, the colour being due to atmospheric or Rayleigh scattering. It was a true harvest moon, and for an age we stared into its depths, lost in our appreciation of but one of nature's many quirks.

As we puffed contentedly, I asked him why red buzzers had taken the fish, but he shook his shaggy head and said, 'It isn't what you fish but the way you fish it'. I looked keenly at him expecting some jest, but the silence grew, so I contented myself with poking him in the eye with my pipe stem.

The Broad Oak coaching inn was built in seventeen hundred and three and stands foursquare and proud on the Old Great North Road that runs through the heart of the village. Tradition has it that a debtor could not be arrested for so long as he chose to remain in the old porch on the frontage. This is thought to have resulted from the right of sanctuary transferring from the nearby Cathedral town of Southwell. Mort attempted it once and was promptly ejected from the said porch by the end of Constable Laurel's steel toe-capped boot, so no other has tried it since. Once an important post house for the shire, it lost prominence with the coming of the new major artery north and now slumbers peacefully as a lovely quaint village watering hole, serving excellent foods via the talented chef Gaston and equally fine wines and ales, plus an under-the-counter cache of Mort's distilled country brews. Inside, in what would have been known as the commons, stands an ancient inglenook fireplace containing a large ornate wrought iron fire basket, in which on this day there roared an open fire of hardwood logs. A sooty brass plaque on the breast bearing the motto *'ignis custodiunt ardentes'* (the flame shall not go out), avowed that Queen Victoria had sought shelter from a storm at the inn one night and that a fire had burned in the grate ever since. Around this cheery blaze sat the piscators from earlier on, listening in rapt and spellbound attention as Roger, in a fine baritone, sang of the wreck of the *Whitby Visitor* and the subsequent launch in foul weather of the *Robert Whitworth* lifeboat. Aided by my beautiful tenor, the Reverend Farthing's average lead and Mort's booming bass, the assembled crowd were visibly moved, with several weeping copiously as the heroism of that night was again brought to life. As pewter jacks banged on table tops for more and cheers awoke the dusky echoes of the hostelry, Mort whispered that we should give them a quick chorus of *Dinah, Dinah, show us your legs*, whereas the vicar wanted to stun the crowd with Bach's *Credo*. However I vetoed any further singing, as my old musical arranger and leader always cautioned that the crowd should leave wanting more, and sure enough, when we declined, a tankard came sailing over to strike Roger a stunning blow to the forehead, poleaxing him to the dusty boards. I placated the now hostile throng by promising a return at some future date and felt sure next time we could charge a fee for performing.

As people turned to sit and continue with their evening, the front door flew open to crash against the wall, as a vision of hell was starkly outlined in the glare from the sodium lamp outside.

CHAPTER TWENTY-THREE

Autumn Leaves

The figure in the doorway took one step and started to fall forward into the tavern. Willing arms caught him before he struck the floor and tenderly carried him onto one of the inn's ancient scrubbed pine tables. From the mangled tripod clumsily twisted about his neck and the roll of film hanging from one of his pockets, I took him to be a photographer. From the lacerations to his face and hands and the tatters to which his suit had been reduced, I further deduced he'd come to harm at the hands of my rancorous sow of a wife and the paws of her evil cur. Gentle hands lifted his head as a libation of the finest Grand Champagne brandy was forced between his lips, and almost immediately, colour flooded to his ashen cheeks as he choked on the fiery spirit.

Between sobs and chokes, it emerged that he had criticised my wife's choice of apparel and make-up for the photography session, not realising it would precipitate such an attack. I could have told him of the thrashing I'd received for once pointing out a little grey in her 'barnet', but instead I patted his hand sympathetically. At one point, he became hysterical and demanded of Constable Laurel that she be charged with assault and actual bodily harm. That doughty officer, however, knew the judiciousness of heading off trouble and suggested a payment for damages, rather than let it be known that he had been bettered by a mere woman. The 'snapper' hesitated as a hat was quickly passed around the pub, and accepted the twenty-seven pounds therein in lieu of blood *gelt*, departing with our good wishes and a pickled egg from under a large glass dome on the bar.

As things returned to normal in the 'commons' room and Roger left for the kitchen to enquire of Gaston the whereabouts of the creamy trout and asparagus risotto, the shadows of Laurel and Doctor Bell fell over me. The copper fixed me with his unblinking stare, nodded once and departed. I knew he'd given me a couple of days' grace to repair the situation or face losing my wife to a probable custodial sentence. I allowed myself a fleeting fantasy of her in prison fatigues before shaking my head and looking in mute appeal to the doctor. He offered me committal for her as being the only option, and it was with a heavy heart that I consented to her being sent to the lunatic asylum next to Fraser's fish farm for psychiatric help. The good doctor said he would forge the second signature required for the incarceration and that all would be well after her treatment. I determined not to allow the sorry affair to spoil my evening and re-entered the commons for a trout supper, strong drink and gaiety.

The next morning I sat up in bed with my head in my hands, nursing an arid tongue and an aching head, and turned to the slattern whiffling and snoring by my side. I almost felt affection for the poor grunting bovine, until I remembered the dreadful assault on the photographer and her impending committal to the asylum.

Susan, our rotund maid, tapped at the bedroom door and entered bearing a tea tray. She sneezed powerfully into my face as she put the tray down, and as she turned to leave I was tempted to propel her through the door with the aid of my shapely foot, but I held my anger, as calm was needed this morning, but I made a mental note to visit some form of retribution on the stupid girl ere nightfall.

Before I awoke the grampus next to me, I mixed a sleeping draft from Doctor Bell with her tea to facilitate the transfer from home to secure mental facility and then leant forward to tweak her nose smartly, bringing her to consciousness. With a roar she awoke and battle was joined as she attempted a knee to the groin combined with a vicious head-butt. Still addled with sleep however, she was easy to read, and I soon had her pinned to the bed in my favoured step-over toe-hold, first learned in a sweaty wrestling booth in Ankara and perfected over many years.

Pinned helpless below me, she stared longingly into my eyes and I felt a fierce reciprocal passion, which we immediately consummated noisily and messily. Later, as the van with the blackened windows crept down the gravelled drive to take her from me, a single tear coursed down my rugged handsome face. I shrugged and continued burning the filthy bed linen and badly soiled nightwear which bore evidence of our recent lovemaking, mulling over the vexing question of how would one know when one had run out of invisible ink.

I decided the best thing for both of us was not to dwell upon her predicament, so I picked up Mort from spinster Arkwright's at two of the afternoon, pointed the softly-burbling Bentley in the direction of Star Lake and enjoyed a few hours of piscatorial bliss. The trout were a joy as they humped through the gentle ripple occasioned by a gentle southerly breeze, and were taking black buzzers, whilst occasionally splashily rising to large crane flies or daddy-long-legs, so that we ceased fishing after a mere two hours, having returned four each, to idle and gossip on the veranda of the lodge. Here we were expertly ministered to by the Moriarty sisters, whose cream teas always lived up to expectation, and whose mini-skirts, displaying large mottled and muscly thighs, never ceased to thrill and amaze. My face must have dropped, however, for Mort questioned my mood and I admitted that the rotten cow to whom I was wed weighed heavily upon my mind. He suggested we visit her that very evening and I slapped my thigh in frustration, for the thought had never crossed my mind.

I removed my stylish, superbly-made brogues in the green oak porch and crept into the darkened cottage, where I stopped and listened. The sound of a fair mezzo-soprano drifted to my ears from the kitchen, and I knew the obtuse and dopey maid Susan was in residence and crooning an old favourite of mine from Puccini's *Madame Butterfly*. I grinned mirthlessly as

I pictured all manner of retribution for her sleight of sneezing upon my noble self earlier that day. Quietly pushing open the old stripped pine kitchen door, I espied her on her knees scrubbing the ancient flags and moved immediately to action. Scooping up the galvanised bucket full of hot water and bleach, I quickly upended it over her and brought it heavily down onto her thick skull. Instructing her to lay tea in the garden room, I then went up to change, light of heart and with a smile on my handsome face.

Later that evening Mort and I clattered lightly up the shadowy tree-lined drive of the institution in my dog cart, drawn by the daemonhound Seyton. Historically used in Europe for delivery and other trades, these carts were prohibited in Britain in the early nineteen hundreds, but were such a novelty with the locals, especially the children, that Constable Laurel never looked twice on the rare occasion of its use.

Strangely quiet and compliant since his mistresses's departure, the cur quickened his pace as we came in sight of the ancient porticoed entrance; I fancied he had caught some essence of my wife on the evening air. Struggling to stop the beast at the door, Mort rapped his cudgel hard against the bony skull of the hound, as to arrive in the hallway complete with cart would have caused somewhat of a stir. As the hound slumped senseless to the gravel, we stepped lightly down and into the reception area.

Et in tota mente iterum (make the mind whole again) was the motto above the desk, where an evil-looking mulatto was languidly peeling an orange, and it was all I could do not to attack as he responded to my enquiry with regard to my wife by flicking his head towards the wards. Mort however, was under no such restraint, and rammed his hoary fist into the man's mouth. The creature obliged us by swooning in his chair as we made our way to the interior.

My wife's lips were tensed in concentration as she put the last double hitch to waxed thread, finishing the beautifully-tied mayfly in the vice that was strapped to her meaty thigh. Applying a drop of varnish to the knot, she admired her handiwork with her head tilted to one side before looking up at the intrusion. She lit up the room with a luminous smile at our entrance, bathing both Mort and me in its warmth. He passed her the bag containing hard-boiled eggs and nuts and backed out of the room, bowing as he went. Never had she looked so attractive, apart from the shaved head and bruises from injections to her sinewy arms, evidence of her treatment. As I took her in my arms I quickly gave her today's fishing report from Star Lake.

She smiled, patted my hand, asked about Seyton and then went to sleep. I was astonished, and hopeful that I may yet take home a normal woman rather than a homicidal Amazon.

CHAPTER TWENTY-FOUR

Healing Hands

The weak and watery sunshine of that first day of November shone through the leaded lights of the master bedroom window onto the sleeping angular features of my beloved wife. I can describe her so because, having been home from the asylum for a week, there had been no violence, petulance, short-temperedness, illogicality or any other negativity associated with the fouler sex. I clung to the hope that she had been cured of her homicidal tendencies, but only the night before I had witnessed her bend the poker with her bare hands in frustration when she realised she would be unable to attend or enter the women's bare knuckle boxing championships that year, and so realised that she was yet to be fully cured.

I was guardedly optimistic though, as Samhain, if you are of the Wiccan persuasion as is she, or Halloween if like me you are Christian, had passed without incident. This was the night when once a year, according to her belief, the dead of the churchyards rose for that wild, frightening festival known as the *Danse Macabre*, but it had come and gone without fuss or ado, so to me this was progress. I was tempted to tweak her ear to awaken her, but resisted as the thought of a quiet breakfast appealed more. Twirling my dressing gown over shoulders, I silently closed the bedroom door, turned and fell over the dog. In an instance the devilish cur was at my neck, long fangs snapping as it sought my jugular. I had it gripped by the throat and began choking the life out of the evil beast as it sought purchase on my arms and legs with cruelly slashing claws, so I did not see the bedroom door open, and only briefly felt the chair smash across my shoulders before losing consciousness.

The noxious combination of bodily odour and rotting meat smote my senses even before I opened my eyes, and I knew I was in the presence of Mort. The meat block on which I lay confirmed my location as the cold room off the larder and kitchen, and the thunderous headache suggested recipience of retribution metered out by the vicious woman of the house for laying hands on her treacherous hound. I sighed as I rose and swallowed the pain-killing libation of powdered willow tree bark and Mort's own sloe gin, and accepted that the cow was back to her old self. The ghost of a grin crossed my classically handsome face as I realised I would not have had it any other way. Pleased as I was to see him, the stench from his carcass and lack of breakfast had my stomach roiling to a degree that made me nauseous, so rolling off the block, I made my way through the pantry and into the kitchen, where I fell over the blockhead maid Susan, who was on her knees industriously scrubbing the floor. As a result I slammed my head into one very hard beech table leg and for the second time in an hour, lost consciousness.

Cuiusvis hominis est errare, nullius nisi insipientis in errore perseverare (anyone can make a mistake, only a fool makes the same one twice)

I awoke to the heavenly aroma of frying rashers, and arising from the window seat where Mort had thoughtfully laid me, I crossed rapidly to the table and sat down to eggs, bacon, mushrooms and sausages, washed down with lashings of Messrs Taylors' finest ground coffee. I felt almost recovered and even forwent the pleasure derived from thrashing the imbecilic blockhead of a girl to listen to the reason for Mort's presence in my fine home.

He looked doleful as he held up his hands. The misshapen, swollen knuckles and joints bore mute testament to the decades of fly-casting grips and holds, including thumb-on, V-style, three-point, and top finger, combining to damage those bear-like mitts that were capable of such sensitivity when fishing. At this time of year, the pain became intense and he all but lost the full use of his hands until a change of the weather, normally after Christmas, and he had come to ask me to accompany him to old Mother Butler's. In country parlance, she was known as a 'wise woman' and everyone in the village was scared of her because she had 'second sight', the supposed power to perceive things that are not present to the senses of the rest of us. She would receive information, in the form of a vision, about future events before they happened, or events at remote locations. She also had a vast knowledge of herbal remedies, which, for a modest consultation fee would prescribe. As modern medicine had failed to cure Mort's hands – Doctor Bell had removed him from his list after Mort had accused the good physic of quackery in the 'commons' of the Broad Oak after failing to affect a cure – he wanted nature to have a go. As far as I was aware, Mother Butler had never harmed anybody, and merely suffered fools very badly. Mort, however, was as superstitious as any native when faced with the esoteric or the arcane, and was incapable of going to see this veteran of the healing arts by himself, so with a sigh, I acquiesced and said we would depart after breakfast and further coffee.

Mid-morning found us flying up the bypass at a steady eighty miles per hour, with the supercharger howling in delight as it pumped compressed air into the cylinders, burning fuel at an alarming rate and increasing power almost instantaneously as I accelerated fiercely out of the bends on the Doncaster road. On two wheels did we leave the main thoroughfare and it was with regret that I eased back on the throttle as we passed through the settlement the old woman we were to see called home. Almost as one left the village on the main street, her ancient lodge-style detached dwelling was the penultimate residence on the right, and I adroitly slipped in through the narrow gates and onto her short drive, cutting the engine, a buzzing silence ensuing.

My ears adjusted to the silence after the roar of the engine, and birdsong and common sounds from the village filled the vacuum as Mort and I clambered out and crunched up a short gravel path to the ornately-carved oak front door, rapping the polished brass knocker in the shape of a fox's head smartly against the wood. The portal opened instantly, revealing a tall, elderly woman dressed in black. Though probably in her late seventies, her face still held the beauty of a younger woman and I guessed years ago she would have been a stunner. Mort obviously agreed. His breathing sharpened as he ran a red serpent's tongue over dry lips.

Alarmed at what the lady might think of us, I cruelly ran the hobnails on the sole of my boot down Mort's shin and heavily onto the tarsals of his foot, eliciting a gasp from him and a slight tightening of the lips from her. She briefly inspected Mort's hands and beckoned him in, asking if I might go round to the rear garden, where I would find her great-grandson in dire need of piscatorial tutorial on the rudiments of casting. I bowed and walked around the house and into the back garden, where a little chap of some eight or nine years, standing next to a canal at the foot of the garden, was struggling with an exquisite three-piece Hardy Bros rod and a floating line.

The next hour was spent happily teaching him to cast an artificial fly onto the waters of the canal, and at the end, we caught an inquisitive perch on a Zulu fly, the bright red tag of a tail no doubt attracting the plucky little predator. I think I made a fisherman for life that afternoon as I showed the little lad how to unhook and return his catch safely to its watery home, and he promised to practise his casting assiduously.

As we walked back to the car, I turned to wave, and saw a black cat delicately walking across the lawn, but no one else save Mort. I suppressed a shiver as he raised his eyebrows and told me what the wise woman had done. We sedately drove back in thoughtful silence, Mort staring vacantly at his ailing hands whilst I wondered what on earth had transpired back there. Still no word passed between us until we arrived back at my magnificent cottage and I directed him to open the garage doors. After stowing the motor in its overnight home, Mort made to leave for the dubious charms of mistress Arkwright, but I mentioned putting the kettle on, and he settled comfortably into the worn old leather armchair in the garden room, steepled his fingers and stared dreamily upwards. I supposed him ensorcelled and quickly took the crucifix from about my neck, transferring it onto his. He sighed, shook his head and passed me it back.

Over a reviving pot of Orange Pekoe tea, he told me of his treatment at the hands of Old Mother Butler. For half an hour he had hair-thin acupuncture needles in various pressure points throughout his body, with many in and around his hands. She told him stimulating these points promoted the body's natural healing capabilities and released endorphins, nullifying pain. He held up his hands and said that for the first time in weeks he was pain-free. She had also given him a cream containing eucalyptus, ginger, turmeric and willow bark for general application and instructed him to drink copious amounts of green tea. When I asked if this would be a permanent cure, he grinned, and said there was one cure, and that would be when he went to the graveyard for good. With that and a wink, he was through the door and trotting down the lane in search of solace in the arms of a certain Miss Arkwright. I watched him go and shivered as I remembered meeting Mother Butler and her great-grandson on that beautiful sunny afternoon.

CHAPTER TWENTY-FIVE

Winter Draws On

The three-month period of the shortest days and weakest sunshine through November, December and January in the Northern Hemisphere is more familiarly known as winter. The freezing temperatures can burst pipes, cover the roads in black ice and produce thick fog, and will just as likely precipitate half a foot of snow in a couple of hours to bring transport to a standstill. In short, it is my least favourite season of the year.

I pressed my nose against the heavily-leaded glass and peered into the garden, hardly focusing beyond the edge of the ancient flagged patio, so thick was the fog. This was not the historical 'pea soup' fogs of London caused by air pollution mixing with mist in the Thames valley, but a mass consisting of extremely cold water droplets or ice crystals suspended in the air at or near the surface of the land that brought village life in the main to a halt. For three days neither I nor the hag had left the house, and feelings were simmering between us. There had already been two scuffles and I wore a plaster above my right eye and carried bruised ribs where she had attempted to stove in my chest with one of her clogs. She had not escaped scot-free however and was limping after damaging her hip, as she had flown over the dining table, landing heavily from a throw I had perfected in the karate schools, or dojos, of Japan. A truce of sorts was holding after we had decided it was preferable to killing one another and we shared a cafetière of the finest Arabica brought in by the stupid and bovine maid Susan. Normally a 'daily', she was currently sleeping at the cottage after failing to get home as she had fallen into the stream that runs alongside the main road in the village on the first night of the fog. I was generously allowing her a small space on the landing and had decided to charge her nothing for her stay. My charity amazes me and is the envy of my peers.

The ogress and I were listening to a haunting version of *'Petite Fleur'*, an evocative clarinet piece played and written by Sidney Bechet, when a hammering came from the massive front door. Susan eventually led in a shivering Mort, complete with heavy topcoat and muffler, who delivered the shocking news that one of our piscators was missing in the fog. It was Squire Elliott, celebrated owner of the slaughterhouse and Manor House, who was absent. The Manor House had existed in the village at the time of the Norman Conquest and mention is made of it in the Domesday Book of ten eighty-six. It is a beautiful house, from the Jacobean-style staircase to the ornate plasterwork ceilings in many of the rooms. It stands sentinel over the village at the crest of a small rise and as such is the most important residence of the parish.

For the owner to have disappeared in the fog was intolerable, and an immediate search for the Squire was the order of the day. Mort informed us that Farmer Wright had organised volunteers to comb the village and its environs, whilst he had wanted to search Star Lake, as the Squire had indicated to his wife that he might do some clearance work down there, followed by a pike fishing session. I frankly doubted the possibility of him being at the water, as to get through the fog would have been troublesome to say the least, but Mort pointed out the Squire's fascination for the pike and I had to agree, so I flung on my greatcoat and glared at the Gorgon who sat toasting her feet against the open door of the log burner, oblivious to the peril of one of our own. The cur Seyton growled warningly as he interpreted this as a threat to his mistress, and I pulled Mort away, as he had started to advance on the warlike dog. The enmity that existed between them would have to wait, as the safety of Elliott was of paramount importance.

We decided transport might be needed should the squire be injured, and the Bentley wheezed lustily before roaring into life as Mort lit two timeworn lanterns before marching smartly out of the driveway. When we had been caught in fog previously it had proved efficacious to walk down the middle of the road, where he could easily follow the white lines with me at a discreet distance behind in the car, with eyes glued to the twin haloes of light supplied by the beacons. Slavering noisily and wetly on the passenger seat was the Squire's Bassett hound, Hugo, whom we had brought because his nose was legendary; he had actually discovered a truffle once in the local woods, after Bayleaf the gardener's sow Annie was unavailable due to her internment in the farrowing sheds.

The journey was long, almost ninety minutes, and uneventful, save when Mort dropped one of the lanterns onto the road, dowsing his feet in paraffin and igniting it, as the glass surrounding the wick was reduced to shards. With a howl, he leaped and skipped like some mad Berserker (a Norse warrior reported to have fought in a nearly uncontrollable, trance-like fury, though probably without the topcoat, muffler and hobnail boots). With a cry, he leapt into the ditch by the road and sighed in pleasure as the flames from his footwear were extinguished by the frigid water therein. I laughed until I cried, finally composing myself under his baleful glare as we continued through the fog, entered the fishery and continued down the rough track towards the fishing lodge.

With an oath, Mort walked into the low picket fence surrounding the lodge, painfully banging his legs whilst I turned off the bellowing Bentley and listened to the engine clicking rhythmically as it began to cool. Mort appeared out of the fog bent double and vigorously rubbing his bruised shins as Hugo enthusiastically licked his face, whilst I put his canine harness on and pulled a pair of underpants out of my pocket and held them tightly to his wet nose. The Squire's smalls, most recently cast to the laundry basket and acquired from his wife, were the best clue we could give Hugo to find his master, if indeed he lurked at Star Lake. The hound inhaled deeply of the pants, paused, then threw back his head and gave a lusty howl, simultaneously pulling at his lead. He was immediately away down one of the paths through the trees to the water, dragging me in hot pursuit. Mort, meanwhile, watched our departure, sat down, still rubbing his shins, and drank deeply of an ornate flask containing his five-year specially-distilled parsnip wine.

Festina lente (hasten slowly)

The ignoramus Mort would have translated the above as 'more haste and less speed' and I would have agreed with him as Hugo and I crashed through the bushes to reappear before the lodge, where Mort sat imbibing his potent potage. He poured an amount of the brew into the palm of his hand, bent down, and briskly rubbed it over Hugo's snout. The dog shook his head and sneezed explosively into Mort's face, which became a picture as the excess mucus, goo and saliva from the dog's chaps and nose slowly ran down his craggy face whilst Hugo huffed and gaily wagged his tail. With a sigh Mort wiped the mess from his face and gently wafted the knickers towards the dog. This time there was a thoughtful silence as Hugo digested the diluted information before he turned, put his nose to the ground and trotted off, on this occasion gently tugging at his lead. Mort shook his head in exasperation as he followed me and the dog at a trot into the thick and swirling fog.

As we turned onto the sheep bank I thought I heard the sound of music, breathy and reedy, and sought confirmation from Mort, who said it was the breeze playing through rush, reed and osier, but the dusk was as still as the freezing fog about us, and I became aware of the hair rising on my neck as the dog continued to pull towards a thin stand of trees. Therein, lying in a shallow depression, was Squire Elliott. His ankle was twisted to an impossible angle, giving mute testimony to his inability to make it back to the lodge. I could hardly breathe, for in the fog beside him stood an imposing figure. I caught the sweep of curved horns, the stern, hooked nose between warm eyes that were looking down kindly on the Squire, at the bearded mouth paused above the pan pipes, clearly the source of the strange music I had been hearing.

Mort gave a gasp, making me turn automatically, and when I looked back, the mysterious visitor had gone. I bent down and felt Elliott's pulse in his neck. I was stunned to find how warm he was, as he had obviously been out in the cold for some hours, and for some minutes following I found it difficult to string a sentence together, so great was my shock at what had happened.

Mort was similarly mute as between us we half-carried, half-dragged our companion back to the lodge.

A light breeze began to gently blow and before we got back to the lodge, visibility had improved to fifty yards and more, so that by the time Doctor Bell arrived to our summons, the fog had all but cleared. The Squire was still unconscious as the physician set the ankle, saying he would take him and Hugo, the faithful hound, home and tell the village to call off the hunt. I was desperately tired, and after dropping Mort at Miss Arkwright's, I promptly retired.

We never spoke of that night, Mort, the squire and I. I can think of no reason why we should not, except that this way, none of us could ever be disbelieved or swayed by the others as to what we had witnessed. I have been through that stand of trees many times since, sometimes in near darkness if I have tarried at the fishing, and have worked there by myself, busily pollarding or clearing, and have not had a repeat of anything supernatural. But it can only have been the Green Man who came to Elliott's aid that evening, saving his life and leaving all three of us the richer for the experience.

CHAPTER TWENTY-SIX

A Winter's Tale

On the first day of Christmas my true love sent to me a partridge in a pear tree. The pear shape is suggestive of the heart, and the partridge – remove the head, eat the heart, then drain the blood into a cup of water, combine overnight and drink it the next morning, having given the servants the day off. I shuddered as I recalled this heady mix my foul wife had me imbibe last year as an aphrodisiac discovered in one of her magical tomes. It had worked, but had left me spent until into the New Year – *nihil enim est nihil* (all things come at a cost) – and persuaded never to try it again.

Mort however embraced the belief wholeheartedly and would whoop with joy whenever the said bird appeared in the sights of his gun, as a session of unbridled lust with the spinster Arkwright was the closest he ever came to Nirvana. Now, however in the first week of December, with a high-pressure system sitting above the British Isles, the weather had been gorgeous. It was bitingly cold, but with clear blue skies and sunshine from dawn to dusk, many were the closed season tasks completed at Star Lake. The reeds were cut back, the trees pollarded and all the fishing platforms re-creosoted, and it looked a picture.

As the sun rapidly went down and the working parties left the lake, three figures had lingered and were ensconced in the lodge. Mort and I, along with Constable Laurel, were preparing to stay the night as sentinels, for we had good intelligence that the lodge was to be targeted by burglars. Two nights before, Clarke the builder had been in his cups in the Broad Oak and had overheard two rough-looking coves planning a 'job at the lake'. No doubt they would be after the silver in the trophy cabinet and the large selection of quality tackle stored therein, plus sundry expensive items from the extensively-stocked kitchen. The following day, he had sought out Laurel, and here we were, in the dark, awaiting events.

By the witching hour, heard chiming across the

frosty fields from the pretty little Norman church in the village closest to Star Lake, nothing had stirred and I was getting stiff and bored, whilst Mort and Laurel were happily cradled in the arms of Morpheus, their combined snores and wiffles making the lodge shake. I could stand the inactivity no longer and gently woke the pair for a cup of flask tea, suggesting we take a turn outside to check the environs. Mort nodded agreement, and Laurel told us to reawaken him should anything occur.

Owls cried out nearby as we quit the lodge, the female 'too-witting', the male answering 'too-woo', causing me to start. Mort grinned, slung his poacher's gun on his shoulder and was off into the darkness. I patted the holster which held my Webley Mk. 6 top-break revolver with automatic extraction and silently followed.

Within ten minutes of walking the lake grounds, my hands, face and feet were frozen. I remembered the first time I met my loathsome wife. My hands were freezing then as I fished for winter pike in the Trent, and she was sitting on one of the supports of the famous bridge of that name, dangling her enormous hairy feet in the river. She cocked an eye at me, then I cocked an eye at her, and there we were, cockeyed.

Mort fared no better, as I could hear his teeth chattering like castanets. I was pondering on being outside for possibly another half-hour when Mort suddenly cried and brought his gun up to his shoulder. A loud retort sounded and smoke belched from the eight-bore fowling piece, this description being based upon the number of lead balls fitting the bore required to make up one pound of lead. His preferred campaign weapon is therefore a large-bore shotgun propelling a two-ounce projectile capable of stopping an elephant. Yet his target was no flying pachyderm but a screeching white horror that made me throw myself to the ground and block my ears. Mort rolled me over and I asked him in God's name what he had shot, to which he solemnly said, with shaking limbs, he had struck the angel of death, for which he would suffer for all eternity.

On tottering legs did we approach the corpse and identify it as a large white swan, stained by a large crimson hole in the breast. I sat on the grass in relief as Mort smiled humourlessly. The swan is revered in Hinduism, and is the sacred bird of Apollo; the god is often depicted riding a chariot pulled by swans in his ascension from Delos. All unmarked swans in open water belong by law to the Queen, though she exercises her ownership only on certain stretches of the Thames and its surrounding tributaries. Notwithstanding, we both were of the opinion that we had probably broken some Crown Law and would suffer accordingly.

Mort became industrious as he does in times of stress, whereas I sat and fretted. He wrapped the bird in a tarpaulin and secreted it in the boot of the Bentley. I awoke Laurel with a cup of tea, whilst Mort fried succulent rashers of bacon on the stove recently blown into life, and with a goodly scrape of English mustard lifted both spirits and temperatures.

Laurel pronounced the night a failure and stated that the crooks would not come now, then tottered away up the lane and away from the lodge on his ancient service bicycle. I poured out more tea into battered enamel mugs as Mort produced his briar and special tobacco pouch. The leaf in question is grown in Miss Arkwright's hothouse, but unknown to her, it is illegal, and can carry a term in prison for its use. Thankfully Mort uses it rarely and never shares it. His crop produces a feeling of euphoria, stimulating brain cells to release the chemical dopamine. More pertinently he experiences heightened sensory perception and has in the past come up with innovative solutions to difficult situations, so I was hopeful we would not end up in the Tower because Mort had slain one of Her Majesty's pets. I paced up and down the lodge in a blue funk whilst he puffed and sighed and rolled his eyes vacantly.

I heard footsteps on the veranda and spun as the door opened, revealing none other than the stout and stolid Constable Laurel, who after sampling one lungful of the sweet, sickly smelling aroma wafting about the room, drew his truncheon and charged.

Twenty-four hours later, after it was deemed that Mort should have recovered from his felonious intake, Laurel literally kicked us out of the village police station, a house with a single cell attached to the rear. The pain from his steel-capped hobnail boot coursed through my derriere as we were catapulted into the street, bailed to appear before magistrates in the new year, by my wife, who troubled not to remain, but departed immediately in her ancient, smoke-belching Land Rover. We repaired to the Broad Oak, where I tried to lighten the mood with witty observations such as the sailor who announced on his eightieth birthday 'aye matey', and recounted how when I told my wife she was drawing her eyebrows too high, she looked surprised.

Mort grabbed me by my ears preparatory to delivering a thunderous head-butt when he was stopped mid-assault as the pub door flew open and Roger the landlord literally capered in. When asked about the source of such gaiety, he proudly stated he had been retained to provide the Christmas dinner at the police headquarters to the north of the village, just off the Doncaster road. Mort put me down and mildly asked our host what was to be the centrepiece of the feast. On hearing that Roger's chef, Gaston, was planning a large turkey dinner, Mort grinned evilly and said he had the perfect bird.

The hall at the cottage was heavily decked with boughs of holly, and everyone was jolly as Mort's sloe gin and strong elderflower wine flowed as free as the pair of us now were. To the amazement of Constable Laurel, the police had dropped all charges due to lack of evidence. He was said to have been put on parole for the way he had handled the alleged crime, rushing in with swinging truncheon rather than methodically collecting evidence, and for some time Mort and I would walk warily around the fellow.

The antique refectory table groaned under the weight of a mass of foodstuffs, as we had also won the police Christmas lottery giant hamper, without, it would seem, purchasing a ticket. The largesse was to end there however, as when Mort had gone up to the headquarters earlier in the day to ask for an allowance of alcohol to be delivered for the Christmas eve party, he had received a black eye and a ride back to the village, where he was ejected forcefully from a moving patrol car onto the village green, to roll unconsciously into the pond. A passing Moriarty sister had retrieved him from the water and revived him with the kiss of life, although it took two villagers to remove her mouth from his.

A scream from the kitchen brought my mind back to the present; Mort's hands were no doubt roving again over one of the luckless women within reach, and I shook my head and smiled as with cudgel in hand I went in search of the old rogue.

Epilogue

I leaned back on the old oak bench next to the path that ran through the graveyard to the rear of the church, allowing the early spring sunshine to warm my upturned face for a few moments. Turning my head slightly, I looked with wet eyes at the newly-erected gravestone under which my friend for over half a century lay. The carving was neat and precise and would say a great deal about Mort when those who knew him personally were no more; a kind of immortality that would appeal to his sense of humour:

There's girls out there who say they will, and then
they say they won't

*There's also girls who say they do and then they say
they don't*

*The girls out there I love the most, and I think that
you'll agree*

*Are the ones that don't say much at all except the
words 'we'll see'.*

I had first heard that little ditty many years ago when
we were in our cups at the Broad Oak, and my mind
effortlessly whirled back over the years to a time when
Mort was still alive and lusty. Roger the Landlord had
turned the key at closing time, and a small party had
continued to chat and gossip and drink. About
midnight, we began to get a little maudlin and I was
ready for the short stagger up Main Street to the
splendid cottage I call home when a soft, reedy voice
spoke from the little stool next to the inglenook
fireplace in the 'commons'. I would not have described
Todd, our obtuse and senseless postman, as a
romantic, but everyone in the room paused and
thought on the words he spoke as he slipped
unconsciously to the sticky, beer-stained floor. Mort
pronounced the words 'most fit' and remarked that
that was the kind of poetry he would like to adorn his
headstone.

Mort, having survived mustard gas in the trenches

and latterly pepper spray from the police, was a seasoned soldier, but he had finally succumbed to pneumonia, that condition which is known also as the 'old man's friend' as the sufferer often lapses into a state of reduced consciousness, slipping peacefully away in his sleep to bring a dignified end to a period of often considerable suffering. Doctor Bell and I were at his bedside at the end, along with his wife, the former spinster Arkwright. He had made an 'honest woman' of her some fifteen years previously, and some said, with copious amounts of dew in the eye, that it was fitting that a love as deep as theirs deserved the sanctity of such a joyous union. In fact Mort told me he could no longer outrun jealous husbands and boyfriends, nor hang from window ledges or scale backyard fences as he had in his youth, due to an increasingly painful arthritic hip, but he was wondrously frank and honest that he really did like the old girl, and if any woman had to be his wife, then she would do. What a man and what a lover. When I recall that depth of romanticism, I am in awe of him.

The wedding was held in August, as that was generally held to be the most difficult month of the piscatorial calendar. Fewer trout were caught then than at any other time of the season, and Mort was quite right to prioritise thus. The nearly-wed Arkwright girl railed at this, but she desisted after

Squire Elliott offered her half a lamb from the slaughterhouse at a reduced price per pound.

My wife, the cow, was asked to be Matron of Honour, with the Moriarty sisters as bridesmaids. I stood in our lounge with my lip curled, watching the three horrors sashaying and swaggering in their new outfits, as full of themselves, like Russian dolls. I remarked that it only required Cinderella in attendance, as we already had the Ugly Sisters. The Moriartys stood suddenly still with red faces turned downwards, but my wife attacked. Throwing back her head preparatory to delivering a thunderous head-butt, she lunged at me. I was ready however, and whipped the ornate bed-pan from off the chimney breast, bringing it in an arc to strike her ear. She stumbled and I quickly knelt, hauling the artfully crafted Moroccan rug from under her and catapulting her into the sisters. As all three went over in a flurry of tangled briefs, I was away and down the short gravelled drive like a ghost at cock-crow, almost colliding with Mort coming up Main Street in his jingle (a small horse cart), in this case being pulled by Albert, Mort's middle-aged donkey. He could not afford to keep a horse, but tethered Albert down by the tithe barn, where the sturdy little steed was constantly fed and petted by the children from the village. Whenever I passed Albert's little corral, I grinned at the long, straight ears that protruded through holes cut into one of the old bowler hats periodically cast aside by the Brigadier, and now worn at a suitably rakish angle to keep the sun off Albert's head.

I now gasped and leapt into the chariot and bade Mort make all speed, as in all probability we were to be pursued by three likely armed and dangerous harpies. He understood and quickly flicked the reins. Albert responded intuitively to the possible danger that suddenly charged the air, leaned mightily into his traces and was off up the road at a handsome six miles per hour. I knew we would be safe up at Frasers' fish farm, for if she pursued at all it would be towards Star Lake, so with another flick of the reins we headed north at the crossroads on the edge of the village.

Fraser welcomed us, noting our somewhat frazzled appearance and equally Albert's sides going in and out like bellows but responding with nothing more than a raised eyebrow. I told him of the altercation with Mrs Audley. Drawing his breath sharply, he quickly led Albert and the jingle behind the red-brick outbuildings, for such was my wife's reputation and capacity for violence that the thought of a visit from her had unmanned him in a trice. However, with the donkey now out of sight, he led us down to the stew ponds, where small trout, through time and the ingestion of high protein pellets, became bigger, and where prying eyes could not see us from the road. Here we spent a relaxing couple of hours feeding the fish.

Later, Fraser produced a half-dozen large potatoes which we roasted in his garden incinerator. Liberally smeared with yellow salty butter and dusted with cracked black pepper and sea-salt, they were sublime. Sprawled in old deckchairs, we sipped strong parsnip wine and watched the stars come out, then thanked Fraser for the sanctuary as we mounted the jingle, pointing Albert back towards the village and Nemesis. Mort asked me to be his best man and I hugged him and said yes. A mistake, as the stench of his unwashed carcase had me gagging and heaving for some moments, until Albert broke wind lustily ahead of us, cleansing the air as a *pot-pourri* might.

Fugietis nemine persequente reus (the guilty flee when none pursue)

There was no enraged Gorgon at the gate as Mort dropped me off. I plodded up the cottage drive listening to the clatter of Albert's hooves becoming fainter as Mort sped to the waiting arms of the spinster Arkwright. Only then did I notice a particular car parked in front of the magnificent green oak porch, a nineteen thirty-five Lagonda Carlton to be precise. A very special, very expensive car that belonged to my wife's Uncle Samuel, warlock and occultist.

All round, he is a dangerous guest to have on the premises. He is tall and cadaverous and looks as if a good meal might kill him, and he is completely bald. An irritating habit of constantly nodding after a reptilian fashion makes me want to punch him repeatedly in the head, but I dare not. One must not touch a person of power or offer him food or drink of any kind. Whilst he was there as my cow of a wife's invited guest, I would walk extremely warily around him, with a container of salt in one pocket and mercury in the other for protection against evil.

Inside the cottage, he surprised me as to the reason for his visit. He informed me that he was there to see Mort married. I remembered, years ago, Mort warning Samuel off when I was tempted to use magic to catch a huge pike, but I could hardly believe he would have waited all this time to extract some kind of revenge upon Mort's person.

Samuel read my mind, possibly literally, and assured me of his selfless reasons for attending. With that and a swirl of his black cape, he retired to bed. I felt a presence behind me and turned to see my wife attired in a see-through knitted green bodystocking. The light from the standard lamp behind outlined every knot and wrinkle of her body, and my heart and stomach sank as an unwelcome longing coursed through my every joint. I hated her and wanted her in equal portions. In one hand she held a leaded cosh, in the other a bottle of baby lotion. Which was it to be, her eyes demanded? I chose the latter.

The next morning, my body a trembling and aching wreck, I was out in the garden burning the bed linen, yet again, after a night of passion spent with the she-devil when Mort arrived with details of the wedding: a bachelor party at the Broad Oak, complete with projectile vomiting and with light damage sustained to the premises. Two days later, a traditional wedding at All Saints Church, followed by the feast to be held at Star Lake with all the village invited. The requisite catering performed by the Moriarty sisters also seemed an eminently good plan.

Mortimer Aloysius Sykes and Mary Arkwright were married on August twenty-fourth. Apart from the titters in church over Mort's middle name, everything went as smoothly as silk. I stand corrected (in my orthopaedic shoes), as I had expected all manner of plagues to descend upon the happy couple, but happily the sun shone brightly and warmly as we all repaired to the lodge at Star Lake to conclude the day's events. Mort and I stood on the porch watching the swallows pluck flies out of the air while enthusiastic trout did likewise to those trapped in the surface film, and then we turned to go in for the meal. It was a cold collation, with a large monkfish as the centrepiece – an incredibly ugly fish, with only the tail edible. I looked at my foul wife and opened my mouth to speak, but I winced as Mort's hobnails scraped painfully down my shin. He shook his head in warning and we sat down to eat.

But then at my side Mort coughed, spluttered and began choking. His face, normally red and mottled, turned blue, and then purple, his hands clutching his throat as he gasped desperately for air. His boots drummed on the floor and he wheezed and looked at me beseechingly.

Everyone in the room froze except for uncle Samuel. He literally picked Mort up and threw him onto the table, scattering plates and bowls alike. Loosening his collar, he plunged three straightened fingers into his throat at the side of the Adam's Apple. Blood welled about the digits and Mort moaned hideously. I grasped a long-tined fork and plunged it deep into Samuel's shoulder in an attempt to stop this assassination of my dearest friend, but he turned his head and his eyes bored into mine. They were yellow, slitted and cat-like, and as he pulled the fork from his upper body, he said it hurt and told me to desist from any further action. He casually tossed the fork in the direction of the younger Moriarty and returned to working on Mort.

I was rooted to the spot, for he now gave a gasp of satisfaction and held aloft a section of gristle and bone from the monkfish that had lodged in Mort's throat. Pressing his Egyptian-cotton handkerchief to the bloody operation site, he bade Mort apply pressure to the wound and lightly hopped off the table. With eyes now normal, he bade us all goodnight, and arm-in-arm with his niece, he swept out of the lodge and into his car.

The mood soured, the party began to break up and people started to go home. Everyone leaving shook hands with Mort and embraced his wife until we three remained, along with the Moriarty sisters banging pots in the kitchen. I drove the newlyweds home in the Bentley and sat with the engine idling and purring outside their cottage as Mort prepared to carry his new wife over the threshold, lest the bad luck and evil spirits that congregate outside the door should take her virginity. I heard a disc in his back crack as he tried to lift the podgy woman, so his wife and I rolled him over the threshold in a wheelbarrow and I bid them goodnight.

Back at my cottage, my wife had gone to bed and Samuel had left for home. I lingered over a beautifully aged potato and turnip brandy, a Christmas present from Mort, and thought about Uncle Samuel. Some little time after the guests had left, Mort had removed the compress from his neck and washed away the blood. There were no puncture wounds, nothing apart from slight bruising. Samuel had performed psychic surgery and had saved Mort's life, of that I was sure.

Possibly the occultist had been at the wedding after having been made aware by arcane means of some imminent danger to Mort, and had interceded on his behalf in repayment for the times Mort had helped me. I don't know, but I would still walk with care in the future around my wife's uncle.

With a start, I realised I'd been wool-gathering, and shivered. The temperature in the graveyard had plummeted as the sun had crept lower in the sky, darkening the cemetery and lengthening the shadows cast by the yew trees over God's acre. I got up a little painfully and slowly from the bench and set off towards the warm glow from the newly-lighted windows of my cottage across Main Street

I started as I heard a sudden chuckle from behind. Mort! My heart leapt and I spun round, crying out his blessed name, but only the gravestones standing silent sentinel met my gaze, and with one last look towards Mort's final resting place I trudged wearily home.